Vivi started to sway to the music in her seat. It was hard not to stare. She sat up straight. "You know what? I think we need to dance."

"Dance? Now?"

She was already standing as she answered. "Yep. You're being spontaneous, right?"

Without waiting for an answer, she strode to the dance floor. What choice did he have but to follow her?

The cocktail must have been stronger than he thought. For after the second or third number, Vivi was somehow in his arms as they moved to the music.

Zeke forgot about the circumstances that had led them to this moment. None of it mattered. Vivi felt right in his embrace, fit perfectly up against him. They'd only just met, but everything about holding her felt familiar. Like she'd been in his arms his whole life, like she belonged there.

Dear Reader,

New Orleans was one of the most memorable cities I've ever had the pleasure to visit. The music, the friendly residents, the glorious Mississippi all left a lasting impression. Not to mention the delicious food!

But there was something else about the city. Something I couldn't quite put my finger on. Then on one of my outings, I visited a quaint little gift shop. I admitted to the proprietor that I was a little lost and not quite sure how to get back to my lodgings. I would have to call up one of those annoying map apps to return. She told me that NOLA has an energy about it, and I should follow that energy to get my bearings. That was one of the many experiences that led me to decide I had to set a book there. The city has an energy, all right. So do the people who live there.

I knew my heroine had to be a daughter of New Orleans—a free spirit who follows her heart despite the risks. And the hero would have to be someone completely opposite. Someone who abides by the rules and lives a life guided by structure and routine.

Vivienne Ducarne and Ezekiel Manning know they have nothing in common. But that fact doesn't seem to impede the intense attraction they immediately feel for each other despite a rather contentious first meeting. Their search for a missing heirloom takes them out of New Orleans and to two of the other most romantic spots on earth. Soon, they can no longer ignore their feelings as they start to fall in love.

As the saying goes, opposites attract.

I hope you enjoy Zeke and Vivi's adventure.

Nina

Around the World with the Millionaire

Nina Singh

HARLEQUIN

Romance

HARLEQUIN®

Romance™

Recycling programs
for this product may
not exist in your area.

ISBN-13: 978-1-335-40697-2

Around the World with the Millionaire

Copyright © 2022 by Nilay Nina Singh

Harlequin Enterprises ULC
22 Adelaide St. West, 41st Floor
Toronto, Ontario M5H 4E3, Canada
www.Harlequin.com

Printed in U.S.A.

Nina Singh lives just outside Boston, Massachusetts, with her husband, children and a very rambunctious Yorkie. After several years in the corporate world, she finally followed the advice of family and friends to "give the writing a go, already." She's oh-so-happy she did. When not at her keyboard, she likes to spend time on the tennis court or golf course. Or immersed in a good read.

Books by Nina Singh

Harlequin Romance

How to Make a Wedding

From Tropical Fling to Forever

Destination Brides

Swept Away by the Venetian Millionaire

The Marriage of Inconvenience
Reunited with Her Italian Billionaire
Tempted by Her Island Millionaire
Christmas with Her Secret Prince
Captivated by the Millionaire
Their Festive Island Escape
Her Billionaire Protector
Spanish Tycoon's Convenient Bride
Her Inconvenient Christmas Reunion
From Wedding Fling to Baby Surprise

Visit the Author Profile page
at Harlequin.com for more titles.

To all those who don't fit the regular molds, who live their lives full of spirit.

And to all the polar-opposite types who love them.

Praise for
Nina Singh

"A captivating holiday adventure!
Their Festive Island Escape by Nina Singh is
a twist on an enemies-to-lovers trope and is sure
to delight. I recommend this book to anyone....
It's fun, it's touching and it's satisfying."

—*Goodreads*

CHAPTER ONE

A PIECE WAS MISSING. A very valuable piece.

Zeke Manning pulled out the inventory list that had originally been prepared for him when the estate was first appraised years ago. Then he compared it once again to the items on the antique mahogany desk in front of him. Yep, something was very, very wrong.

Biting off a curse, he brushed a wayward strand of hair off his forehead. He was here as a personal favor. As the owner of his firm, he never really did fieldwork as an estate attorney anymore. This was supposed to be a quick and easy task coupled with a friendly visit to one of his grandmother's oldest and dearest friends. But now it appeared he had a problem on his hands.

Hopefully, it was merely a simple misunderstanding. Maybe Esther knew exactly where the antique necklace was. She might even have it on her person and had merely neglected to tell him. Esther wasn't remembering much of anything these days.

Well, there was only one way to find out. With a sigh of resignation, Zeke made his way out of the study and toward the parlor, where Esther Truneau, patriarch of the once prominent and highly regarded Truneau family of New Orleans, was taking her afternoon tea.

He arrived to find one of the housemaids pouring tea for her out of a delicate ceramic teapot into a porcelain cup. The aroma of fresh-brewed Earl Grey hovered in the air.

"Hello, Esther," he said after clearing his throat to get her attention. He'd found out the hard way upon his arrival that she was rather easily startled.

She looked up from her cup upon hearing his voice. Zeke paused and waited for the confusion in her eyes to clear. When it finally did, a warm smile spread over her lips.

"Zeke, dear. I'd forgotten you were here."

Zeke made sure to hide his concern. He'd suspected as much. He'd have to follow up with a medical professional to make sure she was getting the proper care and attention for what he suspected had begun a while ago. Returning her smile, he pulled out a newly upholstered chair across from where she was sitting on a love seat.

Without asking, the young lady waiting on

her retrieved a cup from the bottom of the serving cart and poured for him. She set the tea on the coffee table by his side, then gave him a quick smile before leaving the room.

"Esther," he began, his focus fully on the matron who had been one of his beloved grandmother's dearest friends for decades. "I was hoping we might have a little chat."

"Of course, dear. It's so nice of you to visit. Are you in New Orleans on a business trip, then?"

This wasn't good. She'd clearly forgotten the reason he was here. Suddenly, his trip to New Orleans had gone from performing a quick favor for his grandmother's dearest friend to a wellness check that would require further follow-up. As far as he knew, Esther had no relatives in the States.

He leaned forward to make sure he had her full attention. "Esther, you asked me here, remember? After speaking with my grandmother."

She blinked up at him in confusion. Which was answer enough, of course. Finally, she seemed to gather some clarity.

"Oh, yes. Norma mentioned you were coming. That was today, then, was it?"

Zeke summoned his patience and responded as gently as he could. "It's today. That's right.

You asked if I would come over and inventory the house and other properties to get an updated valuation of the estate."

Esther blinked again. "I did?"

Zeke nodded. "Yes. After speaking with Norma."

"I know Norma!" She clapped her hands together then patted his knee. "You're her grandson, aren't you? She looked after you and your sister."

Zeke couldn't believe this was turning into an unwanted trip down memory lane. He simply nodded.

"She was so intimidated, you know," Esther continued. "I remember her telling me how anxious she was about having to raise two preteens at her advanced age. We spoke on the phone about it almost daily."

"She did quite well with us," Zeke answered, not voicing the added thought that Grandmother had done much better than her daughter, who had abandoned Zeke and his sibling after destroying the family.

"Norma said you could help me get my affairs in order with the house."

"That's why I'm here, Esther," Zeke said, as gently as he could manage.

"How kind of you. Carry on, then."

Zeke cleared his throat. "Esther, we need to have a chat first."

"A chat about what exactly, dear?"

"Your estate. Or to be more specific, some of the pieces that belong to the estate."

"Pieces?"

How was he to put this without making her overly upset? Zeke couldn't guess how it might have happened, but Esther had managed to lose an extremely valuable item. Or it had somehow been taken. Not the kind of news he relished delivering to a nice little old lady. "Yes, I'm afraid I've run into something of a snag. An item is missing, Esther. A very valuable item."

Some clarity seemed to appear in the blue depths of her eyes. "Valuable, you say?"

"Very valuable."

She lifted an eyebrow. "What kind of piece?"

"Jewelry. A necklace from sixteenth-century France. Your records say it had been passed through several generations of the Truneau family. I'm afraid there's no sign of it in your possessions. While the paperwork says it should be right here in your house safe."

Her eyes finally lost all signs of cloudiness and grew wide with shock. For the first time since Zeke had walked through Truneau Manor's doors this morning, Esther appeared completely lucid.

"Oh, dear. That's quite bad, isn't it?"

Zeke took her hand gently and patted it re-assuringly.

"I'm sure it was a simple misunderstanding. Probably merely a mistake," he insisted in an attempt to quell her fears. He hadn't meant to alarm her.

"I just need your help to determine exactly what might have happened to it."

She blinked at him once more. "Of course."

"Can you think of the last time you might have seen it?" As clichéd as the question seemed, Zeke figured it wasn't a bad way to start an investigation.

Esther shrugged, her forehead scrunched in concentration. "All the valuable jewelry is always under constant lock and key. Only taken out to be polished, which I only allow my most trusted staff to do. People I've employed for decades."

First off, he would need to look into all her staff members. He really didn't want to get the authorities involved until he was a bit clearer as to what was going on here, exactly. And there were other avenues to explore still.

"I see. Is there a chance you might have lent it out?" he asked her. "Temporarily? To a gallery or museum perhaps?"

Esther immediately shook her head. "Oh, no. I don't lend out valuables."

Zeke racked his mind for another avenue to pursue when her next words stopped him. And they sent alarm bells ringing in his head.

Without any irony whatsoever, Esther added, "I have been known to give things away occasionally, however."

Fifteen minutes later, Zeke had a name and was looking at a photo online of a dark-haired, brown-eyed woman with shoulder-length curly hair. She wore dramatically dark eyeliner and appeared to be in her mid-to-late twenties.

All in all, she looked like she might very well fit the type. A type he knew all too well. If Zeke's suspicions were correct, he was looking at a photo of the kind of person who would take and take until there was no more left to give.

"I'm almost positive he'll propose this weekend. What do you think, Vivi?"

Vivienne Ducarne flipped six cards in a semi-circle on the velvet table cover between her and the client who came in every Thursday for a reading. Sally's question this morning was the same as it had been all too often in the past.

"Well, let's look at what the cards say, shall we?"

Sally McNeill had become a regular customer over the last several months, ever since meeting Lance. Or was it Luke? Vivi knew she should pay better attention, but the man's name hardly seemed to matter. Sally usually referred to him as her stud muffin.

Sally had made her way into Lucien's Magic Shop and Gift Store the morning after their first blind date to see where things might lead between them. So far, the two of them had been enjoying a whirlwind romance according to Sally's rather TMI descriptions. The woman was more than ready for the relationship to move on to the next level. Vivi didn't have the heart to tell her that she just didn't see that happening in any of her readings so far.

Of course, she wasn't about to tell Sally that. Not directly, anyway. It would crush the other woman's excitement. Why dash her hopes?

Vivi pointed to a card in the center. "The Empress. That card could mean a few different things."

The other woman released a long sigh. "Ooh, like what?"

"Well, in your case, I think it means a strengthening of bonds. Growth in your relationships in general."

Sally clapped her hands in front of her chest. "That's great. I knew it!"

Before Sally could get too worked up, Vivi pointed to the card right of center. "The Seven of Pentacles. That's something of a cautionary card."

Sally's eyebrows drew together. "Caution-ary?"

"It usually refers to patience and persever-ance. A message not to try and rush things, but approach matters with more of a long-term mindset."

Sally seemed to deflate in her chair, her smile faltering. "Huh. Long-term?"

Vivi merely nodded.

"So what do you think, then, Vivi?" Sally repeated. She asked that question a lot, in fact.

Vivi tapped her chin. "I think you're in store for some good tidings coming your way. A lot to look forward to."

Just like that, the smile reappeared.

"The cards seem to be advising you to try and be a bit patient. For now," Vivi reassured her.

Ten minutes later, after some more questions from Sally and a bit of random chitchat, her cus-tomer left. Sally seemed content with what fate had chosen to show her today through the tarot cards. A lot of folks looked down upon oracle cards, such as tarot or runes, even in a city as spiritual as New Orleans. But Vivi saw it as a craft, an art almost. Not only did Vivi interpret what the cards displayed in a manner that felt relevant to her clients, but she also knew she was just as talented at providing conversation or simple reassurance. Sometimes, her clients just needed someone to talk to.

Esther Truneau came to mind. Vivi had been giving the nice old lady personal readings for the last several months. Sometimes she wondered if Vivi was the only source of meaningful human contact the older woman had in her life. Her staff seemed to mostly ignore her when Vivi was there.

Vivi packed up the cards and started tidying the shop. It was a pretty slow day, with not too many shoppers strolling in, and Sally had been her only prebooked appointment.

The chimes above the door sounded as someone entered.

Vivi looked up with a smile to greet the customer—finally, some action. Slow days bored her to tears.

Her breath caught in her throat before she could offer a greeting. The man walking in was strikingly handsome. Which was saying a lot for someone who worked in a magic-and-gift shop in the heart of one of the world's most famous cities. This area drew visitors from all over the world.

Tall with jet-black hair and chestnut eyes, he had a strong jawline and ruggedly sharp cheekbones. He wasn't overly muscular, but was fit and toned.

He obviously wasn't any kind of typical tourist. That much was abundantly clear. Dressed in a black collared shirt, which appeared to be silk, with pressed gray pants that had a perfect crease line, he seemed to fit the picture of an accomplished, successful businessman.

So what was someone like him doing in a quaint tourist trap of a shop in the middle of the morning? Had he gotten lost on his way to a high-powered acquisition meeting?

Vivi shook off the beginning of a giggle and cleared her throat. "May I help you find something, sir?"

His eyes narrowed on her and she suddenly had the strange urge to duck behind the nearest counter. A shiver of iciness ran along her spine. His gaze was clearly not a friendly one. And he certainly didn't appear to like what he was looking at.

She wasn't imagining it. She didn't even need her so-called "seer" skills to be able to tell as much.

Working hard not to bristle at his hostility, she forced a smile on her lips. "Was there something in particular you were looking for?"

"Oh, I'd say so," he answered with a cryptic clip in his tone.

What was that supposed to mean? "I beg your pardon?"

"Are you Vivienne Ducarne?" he asked without any hint of cordiality.

Vivi's heart pounded in her chest. He had to be a cop, maybe a detective. But why would an officer of the law be dressed as impeccably as he was?

Ha! Like that was the most pressing question she had at the moment. A better one would be what would a cop want with her?

Her days of hiding from the law were well in her past. She'd left that part of her life behind years ago, when she'd finally cleaned up her act and wised up enough to dump the charming yet toxic ex-boyfriend who'd led her down so many objectionable paths. There was absolutely no reason she could think of as to why a law-enforcement officer might be seeking her out at this moment in time.

But she realized her mistaken assumption the more she studied him. Now that she took a good look at him, she knew one thing for certain. He was no cop. Every inch of him screamed that he was a professional man with privilege and clout. Just the pants he was wearing would probably cover a beat cop's monthly salary.

So if his visit wasn't about her past, what was it about?

He was staring back at her just as intently.

That's right—he'd asked her a question. Her name. He was still waiting for an answer.

"My friends call me Vivi. So you can call me Vivienne. Not that it's any of your business." She had a question or two of her own. "And who might you be?"

"The name is Zeke Manning. Esquire."

An attorney. She should have known. She'd had to interact with more than enough criminal lawyers in her lifetime. But something told her criminal law wasn't this man's specialty.

"What can I do for you, exactly, Mr. Manning? I gather you're not here for a tarot reading?"

"A what?" He gave his head a shake. "Never mind. You gather correctly. That's not why I'm here."

She tilted her head in his direction, the perfect picture of unaffected patience. But inside, she was a trembling mess. This stranger really had her rattled. The last time someone had looked at her so accusingly, so disdainfully, she'd been a scared teen at the full mercy of the court.

It also didn't help matters that the man looked like something out of a cologne ad in a high-end magazine.

"Then please enlighten me."

"For one, you can start by handing over that which doesn't belong to you."

Vivi summoned all her will and strength to try and get her rapid heartbeat under control. Who was this man? And who did he think he was talking to?

Well, if he thought he could intimidate her, he had another think coming. Vivi had survived and prevailed against far scarier people in her lifetime. Not to downplay his sheer presence, but she knew how to handle bullies.

And this man was clearly trying to bully her.

"I have no idea what you may be referring to, Mr. Manning." That was the absolute truth. The days of being accused of any kind of crime were well in her rearview mirror. Or so she'd thought. "But I think I'd like you to leave."

He quirked an eyebrow. "I can come back with the proper authorities."

What the…? *Authorities?* What was his game? She'd done nothing wrong! Not in the recent past, anyway. And she'd absolutely paid her dues for all that had come before.

Anger and frustration raged inside of her. Along with what she had to admit was a mild curiosity. What in heaven's name was he referring to, exactly? She really shouldn't care. The sooner she got him out of the store, the better she could breathe. He was starting to make her feel really unsettled.

"Like I said, I have no idea what you're talking about. Come back if you feel you must. With whoever you wish to bring." She managed to fill her voice with false bravado somehow, though the prospect of seeing this man again was making her shudder. She wanted to kick herself for feeling even the slightest bit intimidated. She'd handled far worse in her lifetime, including tense questioning in dimly lit rooms by trained officers. There was no reason for this man to make her feel quite so shaken up. It was hard not to feel those old insecurities and fears bubble up to the surface when confronted, but she forced them away.

"But right now, I'd like you gone."

She would not be hassled here, of all places. Lucien's Magic Shop was one of her safe spots. A second home. A haven. It had been so for years. She would not allow this man to desecrate the sacredness of this store.

Too late, a little voice whispered in her mind's ear. The voice was right, of course. She could hardly deny that she was rattled.

Lucien chose that moment to step out from the inventory room, a grave look of concern marking his face. "Vivi? Is everything all right? Is this man bothering you?"

She must have raised her voice when she'd asked this Zeke to leave. Vivi sent a reassuring smile in Lucien's direction. The last thing she wanted was for things to escalate and have her boss involved in some type of altercation.

Something told her Zeke Manning wouldn't shirk away from a fight, physical or otherwise. Lucien wasn't exactly in his prime, or the violent type.

"He was just leaving," she said with clear force, shifting her gaze back to Zeke.

He appeared ready to argue, staring at Lucien intently. Then he gave his head a brisk shake.

Zeke Manning's next words did nothing to alleviate her disquiet, however. "Fine. I'll go for now. But trust me, this isn't over."

He might have overdone it.

Zeke poured an inch of bourbon into a glass from his hotel room's well-stocked bar rack and contemplated the day's events. Perhaps he'd been a bit overzealous in confronting the young lady. He probably should have called a colleague more familiar with this sort of thing. It's not as if he practiced criminal law. His specialty was in estate and trust planning, a completely different field.

Ms. Ducarne's face kept reappearing in his mind's eye. Her expression was as clear as if she stood in front of him at this very moment. If he didn't know any better, he might say she'd looked scared.

Or maybe she was just a good actress and he was being influenced by a pretty face. A *very* pretty face. It had shocked him when he'd first walked into the shop just how attractive she was. The photos he'd found online had not done her justice. She had striking features—dark, almond-shaped eyes and curves in all the right places.

It had thrown him off, he had to admit.

Damn it.

He had no reason to feel guilty. Even if he had been a bit over-the-top. A highly valuable antique was missing. Just because Vivienne Ducarne was attractive didn't mean something ugly hadn't gone down involving her and Esther. Zeke owed it to his grandmother—and to Esther—to uncover the mystery.

He just might have if the shop owner hadn't shown up at that moment. Zeke had never been afraid of a fight and had gotten into more than a few skirmishes in his lifetime. The man had certainly looked ready to defend his employee in any way necessary, despite having several years on him. Not that Zeke could blame him, given what the man must have been thinking if he'd overheard them. At that point, Zeke had figured the best thing to do was leave. He could have told the shop owner the truth about why he was there, but something made him hesitate. He hadn't been quite ready to jeopardize Vivienne's livelihood right then and there. Esther had given Vivienne the necklace, after all.

This isn't over.

He'd actually uttered those very words as a parting warning before he left. How utterly dramatic. Like a scene out of a bad movie.

Still, he refused to feel remorseful. He'd learned the hard way, more than once, that when it came to a certain type of person—the type that had no qualms about taking advantage of others—it was always better to be safe rather than sorry.

Zeke had seen it firsthand, starting when he was only a child, how letting one's guard down could not only destroy the life of those most gullible, but also everyone else within range.

To be trusting was to play the fool.

Zeke had no doubt in his mind that Ms. Ducarne was exactly the type who should make others wary. Sure, he could have handled things better today. But the facts were the facts. Vivienne Ducarne had somehow finagled her way into being gifted a near priceless piece of jewelry.

Well, there was one way to find out exactly what kind of person she was. It was high time he called in a professional.

Zeke pulled his phone out of his pocket and pulled up his contact list. He only called Bill

Wolfson under the most pressing of circumstances. And the current scenario certainly
seemed to qualify.

The other man answered on the first ring.
"Wasn't expecting a call from you, Ezekiel.
What's on the horizon, then?"

Bill was one of the few people who insisted
on using Zeke's proper name. He'd long ago
accepted it as just another of the man's many
quirks. Along with the catch phrase he often
used: *What's on the horizon, then?*

"I could use your help to get to the bottom
of something."

"Hmm. Kind of figured that or you wouldn't
be calling. Any specifics?"

Right. Bill was the type where if you didn't
get right to the point, he would be sure to call
you on it.

"I have a name I'd like you to investigate.
Along with her place of employment."

Zeke heard the other man's resigned sigh over
the tiny speaker. "And I don't suppose you're
willing to share anything more than that? Like
why I'm looking into this person?"

"Not just yet. I'll text you the info you need
for now."

Bill didn't have any more questions. They'd
worked together for a long time now. Knew each
other fairly well.

Zeke clicked off the call and dropped his phone on the hotel-room bureau. There, he felt better already. Bill would be able to uncover some answers for him. Hopefully it wouldn't even take that long. Zeke had enough going on between his responsibilities at the firm and his latest investments. Not to mention the French-winery acquisition that needed his focus before his trip to Provence. He didn't need a headache like Vivienne Ducarne right now.

Speaking of pressing responsibilities… Zeke picked up his cell phone again to check his latest emails and review updates on his pending projects. A message from his grandmother stood out among the others. She'd used several smiley-face emojis as her subject line. He clicked on the body of the message.

Hope you're enjoying New Orleans. Thanks again for handling Esther's affairs personally. She's a true friend who has always been there whenever I needed her throughout the decades.

Zeke bit out a curse and sighed.

He supposed he could do some investigating on his own in the meantime while Bill did his own thing. Looked like he'd have to pay another visit to Lucien's on Bourbon Street. The sooner, the better.

* * *

The magic store was closed when Zeke made his way back there three hours later. A strange feeling of disappointment swelled in his chest— a feeling he didn't want to examine too closely. He was merely disappointed about having wasted his time coming here on a futile errand. He should have called first.

Zeke resisted the urge to swear out loud as his agitation grew. It had nothing to do with missing an opportunity to see *her* again. That would be downright silly. He'd only laid eyes on the woman for the span of a few short minutes. And their encounter could be described as contentious at best. Still, an image of Vivienne's almond-shaped eyes and sparkling smile appeared in his mind's eye, though her smile had faded when he'd confronted her.

No. This impulsive trip had nothing to do with her. He was here for one reason only. For Esther. To make sure she wasn't being taken advantage of.

Surprising, really. The shop seemed to be the only thing shut down as far as the eye could see. Around him the street bustled with both noisy tourists and what appeared to be locals. Jazzy music blared from every direction. A makeshift percussion band performed on the corner, using everything from large plastic buckets to aluminum cans. Neon lights lit up the night in every direction.

Bourbon Street seemed to have an energy Zeke would be hard-pressed to compare to anywhere else he'd been in his extensive travels. Sure, he'd visited New Orleans several times in the past. But he was usually at one business meeting after another before retiring to his hotel room in a quieter part of the French Quarter, only to do it all again the next day before he had to return to Manhattan.

Well, his fact-finding would have to wait another day, at least. Would she even be here if he came back tomorrow? He had no way of knowing if she worked every day. What sort of hours did tarot-card readers keep, anyway? To think, there were people out there who actually paid to have someone interpret what a bunch of cards meant as it pertained to their future. Just another grifter, as far as Zeke was concerned. It was a big clue into this Vivienne Ducarne's character that she made her living off gullible people.

How did Vivienne even happen to meet Esther and grow close enough to the old woman that she was being given valuable jewelry as a gift?

Zeke shook his head in consternation. Perhaps the better question was, why was he so curious about her in the first place? He couldn't deny that something about her had called to him. Even during their brief, rather volatile conversation, everything from her manner to her attire had piqued an interest that he felt rather confused about. His grandmother's affection toward Esther aside, if he was smart, he would wish the elder lady the best, wrap up the appraisal of the estate as best he could and simply wait for Bill's answers about the beguiling Ms. Ducarne while more qualified professionals dealt with the mystery of the missing necklace.

Whoa. Where had that come from? He was thinking of her as beguiling now?

That did it. He had to get out of this city. Maybe it was the bewitching atmosphere. New Orleans was known to have a certain mystical energy. That's what the locals always said, anyway. He'd never given it much credence or thought, for that matter, that the city's main attractions involved hexes and paranormal influences.

Or maybe it was simply the strong Louisiana bourbon he'd indulged in back in his hotel room. Zeke didn't know. But he couldn't even recall a previous time he'd ever described a woman as "beguiling." It simply wouldn't do.

He was going to drop this matter. Let the expert investigator deal with it. But as he was turning away from the store window, a colorful flyer caught his eye. A classic-looking tourist steamship floating on the majestic Mississippi River. The poster was an advertisement for a party cruise that featured dinner, an open bar and a live band.

But the image that really drew his attention was a black-and-white thumbnail-size photo at the bottom corner of the paper.

Ms. Vivienne Ducarne was apparently a part of the river-cruise entertainment being offered this evening.

CHAPTER TWO

VIVI'S EARS STILL burned with anger as she made her way down the concrete steps and across the boardwalk to the River Rider steamboat's usual docking spot. She had to find a way to calm down. As part of the evening's entertainment, it wouldn't do to appear furious and frazzled as she sang onstage. Sure, she wasn't even the main act. That would be the jazz band with whom she added vocals on a handful of songs. Still, she would stick out like a sore thumb onstage if she appeared angry or perturbed. The whole atmosphere on the boat was supposed to be one of fun and joviality.

Still, calming down was going to take some work. The more she thought about…that man, whoever he was, the more her ire grew. Who did he think he'd been speaking to?

On top of apparently trying to accuse her of some kind of wrongdoing, there had also been an undercurrent of disdain. People like him always did that—approached her with a dismissive attitude, as if people like Vivi were hardly worth their time. For most of her childhood and teen years, she'd been nothing but a loose bolt in the system. A variable that needed to be addressed and then set aside. No one had been there to look out for her or stand up on her behalf. She'd had to do it all herself, not that anyone bothered to do much listening when she tried to stick up for herself.

The sting of tears burned her eyes before she could fully steel herself against the onslaught of bitter emotion. Hadn't she sworn all afternoon that she was going to do her best to forget about Zeke Manning? She had a job to do, and she couldn't jeopardize this gig. People had paid good money for an evening of entertainment and fun.

Looked like it was a good crowd, too. She could see the line of people waiting to board snake around the dividers leading up to the entrance plank. Not bad for a Thursday evening. Vivi wasn't quite in demand enough to win one of the coveted weekend slots, or even be billed as the headliner on the evenings she was here. But this continued to be a great opportunity for her. With her past, she didn't dare pursue any kind of career that might put her on a national stage. But the opportunity to sing on a busy tourist attraction was the next best thing. Despite the late hours and the occasional overzealous male patron who'd overindulged in the bourbon punch the bartender specialized in, she enjoyed being up there on the small corner stage.

Not surprised you don't have any kind of real job.

The unwanted voice of her last foster father invaded her thoughts before she could stop it. Much to Vivi's dismay, she still ran into the man around town now and again. Their unwelcome conversations always ended with some kind of insult about how Vivi lived her life. As if it was any of the man's business. She'd turned eighteen and aged out of the system years ago.

Real job or not, Vivi was proud that she worked hard at what she did. So what if it was a collection of gigs here and there? Tarot readings and retail sales at the magic shop. Waitressing for the lunch crowd at the Crawdad Café and performing two nights a week on a steamship earned her enough money to pay her rent and buy her groceries. The waitressing even got her a free lunch every afternoon.

It wasn't much. But it was a far cry from the days when she couldn't guess when her next meal would be, or where it would come from. Someone like Zeke Manning had probably never gone hungry a day in his life.

Now, why had her brain drifted back to that insufferable man yet again? The sooner she eradicated him from her mind, the sooner she could get on with her evening. He'd made it clear that they'd be meeting again at some point. That prospect sent an icy shiver traveling up her spine. But she certainly didn't need to dwell on his existence in the meantime. She'd deal with him when she had to.

Or maybe he would figure out she had nothing to hide and be on his way. She may never even see him again. For some inexplicable reason, that notion didn't bring the level of satisfaction it would have warranted. Frustrating as it was, she was a warm-blooded woman. And Zeke Manning was certainly easy on the eyes.

Don't. You. Dare.

How many times in one lifetime could she err on the side of sheer stupidity when it came to men? She'd barely laid eyes on this Zeke, had no business thinking about how handsome he was. Especially not after the way he'd treated her.

By the time she reached the boat and made her way on board, she was still chastising herself. How could she even think about the attractiveness of a man who had just that morning shown up at her place of employment to berate her without so much as an explanation as to why. Handsome though he was.

Stop it.

Anyway, something told her she hadn't seen the last of him by any means. Zeke Manning didn't seem the type to let things go.

The friendly faces of the crew greeted her as she made her way to the staff cabin below deck. The engine slowly roared to life as billows of steam drifted in the air. The excited sounds of passengers as they slowly boarded became louder and louder as the crowd grew. Excitement hummed through her veins as Vivi mentally prepared herself for the performance later this evening. Being onstage made her feel vibrant and alive. Any nervous energy quickly turned to excitement when she let her voice simply take over and she became Vivi the vocal artist.

Some might say she was nothing more than a lounge singer belting out tunes for some extra cash and a few measly tips. But Vivi knew it was much more than that.

Up onstage she became someone else—the music took over her soul, the melody allowed her to temporarily stop thinking about her past and the daily struggle it was to make ends meet, along with all the negativity that had followed her around since childhood.

She forgot about the voices of those people who wanted to belittle her. Vivi doubted herself about many things. But she was certain she could carry a tune. And that she had a voice. Maybe it wasn't one that would make her famous or any real amount of money. She didn't want any of that, anyway. She just loved who she became when she was onstage.

Today, she hoped being up there and performing would allow her to forget about the clear derision she'd seen in Zeke Manning's eyes earlier that day.

He almost missed it. Zeke took a moment to catch his breath as he watched the boarding plank be lifted much too close after he'd just cleared it. He'd never been an impulsive sort. Yet he'd surprised himself by calling a car to make it to the square, then fought the throngs of tourists along the river walk that led to the dock.

But it had been close. In fact, the agent in the ticket booth had been reluctant to sell him a ticket, explaining he'd cut it much too close, that the crew was making the final preparations before setting sail.

It had taken quite a bit of convincing and no small amount of charm to persuade her. Now that he was aboard and the boat was en route, Zeke had to wonder what had gotten into him. How had he ended up on a tourist steamship cruise when he had so much to do? Still, there were worse ways he could be spending the evening than a tour of the Mississippi. Not to mention, it was a dinner cruise and he had to eat, didn't he?

He took a moment to study his fellow passengers. All the coveted spots along the railing had been taken. The smaller tables sat two or three. Most of them were inhabited by lovestruck couples holding hands, or sharing a snack and a drink. One couple appeared to be in the throes of a passionate kiss.

Get a room.

The larger tables were occupied by noisy families with laughing, screaming kids and indulgent parents.

Yep. He was the only person on board who appeared to be here by himself. He hadn't really thought this through. Not that he had any kind of qualm about spending time alone—he just didn't like to stick out. And in a crowd such as the one on the steamship, he stuck out like a sore thumb. A small trickle of discomfort drifted over his skin. He'd spent most of his childhood making sure to attract as little attention as he could, constantly trying to be seen or heard as little as possible.

The least conspicuous thing would be to hang out at the freestanding bar in the center area of the upper deck. He could chat with the bartender. Small talk always came easy for a man who was used to dealing with all manner of clientele. He'd worked hard over the years to perfect the art.

After making his way to the serving area, he pulled out one of the barstools and sat. The bartender approached immediately. He was a tall, wide-shouldered man with a thick ponytail made up of elaborate braids, and his wrists were covered with gold jewelry.

"I know what you want, my man," he told Zeke with a smile, pointing a finger at him. "Our specialty, the bourbon punch."

"You're the expert. I'll take it."

"You're gonna love it, man."

Zeke watched as he walked to the other side of the bar and pulled out a plastic pour container and a gold glass bottle of liquor. He mixed the two expertly then poured the mixture into a tall, frosty glass.

This was good. The bartender was chatty and friendly with a perpetual smile, and it made him feel less like the lonely tourist.

He could always take out his phone, but he didn't want to waste this beautiful evening staring at a small screen. The scene around him was too majestic. The sky was a beautiful, deep shade of pearly blue as the sun got ready to set. Thin, cotton-white clouds formed various patterns above.

"You in NOLA on business?" the bartender

asked, sliding his drink across the wooden surface. The glass stopped expertly in front of him, not a drop spilling over the side.

Zeke nodded. "I am. Thought I'd do something fun while I'm here."

"Good for you," he said. "It's good to explore this city. Too many business people come here and don't bother to check out all the wonderful things New Orleans has to offer. I'm Tomas, if you need anything else," he added with another friendly grin.

Zeke took a sip of his drink. Tomas was right. It was good. A bit fruitier and sweeter than his usual fare, but the tangy flavor hit the spot.

"I'm actually on board looking for someone," he told Tomas. "There's something we need to discuss and we didn't exactly get off on the right foot." Why he'd admitted such a thing to a virtual stranger, friendly or not, he had no idea.

"Oh, yeah? That happens sometimes in life," Tomas offered wisely.

"Wanna talk about it?" Tomas asked. "You can tell me."

Before Zeke could answer, a recently familiar voice sounded behind him. A voice he'd heard echoing in his head more than once over the last few hours.

"Hey, Tomas. Nice night, huh? Could I get a glass of lemon water?"

He wouldn't have thought it possible, but the bartender's smile grew even wider, and a softening Zeke would describe as tenderness washed over the other man's features. Yet another one loyal to Vivienne Ducarne, it seemed. First the shop owner, now the bartender. Her ability to elicit such loyalty reminded him of someone he'd rather forget.

"Coming right up, Vivi."

Taking another large gulp of his drink for some liquid fortitude, Zeke turned slowly to face her, bracing himself for her sure-to-be-volatile reaction. He wouldn't be surprised if the woman chose to fling her lemon water in his face rather than drink it.

It would probably be less than what he deserved.

She glanced past him at first, tilting her head in a friendly nod. She appeared to do a double take a mere second later. Then her focus found his face again. Her eyes grew wide and her mouth fell open.

"You!"

"What are you doing here?" Vivi felt her pulse shoot clear to the sky and the heat of anger travel clear down to her toes. "Are you trailing me?"

Zeke held his hands up in the air, palms facing her. "It's not like that."

Oh, she couldn't wait to hear his explanation, then. Considering he was here now at yet another place of her employment. "Then how is it exactly?"

"I went about things the wrong way earlier today."

She'd say so. "Get off this boat. I want you gone."

His head tilted to the side, one ear nearly touching his shoulder. "Where to, exactly? If you happen to have forgotten, we're on a boat in the middle of one of the USA's longest and deepest rivers."

"A boat you have no business being on. Now leave."

"I would have to jump into the water."

"That suits me just fine." She knew she wasn't making any sense. But shock and trepidation were making it hard to think straight. She hadn't expected to see him here. He'd caught her off guard. She felt frazzled and unprepared. Along with something else she didn't exactly want to name. Heaven help her, she did want to know what his deal was. Why was he after her? She knew without any doubt whatsoever that she wasn't in any kind of danger from this man. Not physically, anyway. With the life she'd led, she could spot such peril miles away. No, he wasn't that kind of a threat.

But that didn't mean he wasn't dangerous.

"Look, I went to the magic shop on Bourbon and it was closed. A flyer on the window advertised that you'd be here."

She gave her head a shake in a futile attempt to clear it. "I'm sorry. How does any of that sound like you're not trailing me?"

Tomas appeared on the other side of the bar with her lemon water. He set it in front of her, but his eyes were trained squarely on Zeke's face. "Is there a problem here, Vivi?" the bartender asked, his voice laced with clear concern.

Great. She didn't want any of her friends involved in whatever this mess was. No one who worked on the boat, the magic shop, or the café knew anything about her past. Except for Bessa, her roommate, who also happened to be her best friend. No one else had a clue.

She wanted to keep it that way.

She took a deep breath to try and calm down. The last thing she needed was any kind of scene here, similar to the one earlier, at the magic store. "Nothing I can't handle, Tomas. Thank you."

Tomas didn't so much as shift his glaring gaze from Zeke. "Are you sure?"

"Yes," she assured him, grateful that he was

looking out for her. It was a strange feeling. She was still getting used to the concept of having friends who actually cared about her well-being. "Thanks."

She couldn't help but laugh out loud when Tomas, with complete and utter seriousness, pointed two fingers toward his own eyes and then one at Zeke's chest. The universal sign that said, "I've got my eyes on you." He lingered a few seconds after the gesture, then finally turned away to attend to other thirsty customers.

"Thanks a lot," Zeke said with a wistful tone, watching the other man retreat. "We were just starting to become friends."

"I find that hard to believe."

He turned back to her and took a drink of his cocktail. "What? That I can make friends?"

Calm and charming. While she was shaking inside. What kind of effect did this man have on her and why? Sure, he was handsome in a striking and disarming way. Tall and dark. Piercing expressive eyes. She'd been right in her earlier assessment. He wouldn't be described as muscular, per se. But he was certainly in shape. He probably belonged to the best gyms and could afford the most exclusive trainers. But there was nothing soft about him. The edge was there. It was in his voice, in his mannerisms. He wasn't the type one wanted to tangle with.

She should probably do her best not to goad him.

Just figure out what he wants and move on with your life.

But she couldn't seem to help herself.

"Let's just say I've yet to see your friendly side," she answered, taking a sip of her water.

He ducked his head. "You have me there. It's why I'm here. I came to find you to say I was out of line. I should have handled our first meeting much better than I did."

"That is a very weak apology, Mr. Manning."

He merely quirked an eyebrow at her. This wasn't a man used to being repudiated in any way, she wagered.

"If you're here to tell me you're sorry," she continued, "then just say it."

The slightest hint of a smile tugged at the corners of his lips. He lifted his drink to her in a salute. "I'm sorry."

Before she could feel any kind of satisfaction, he added, "For the way I went about things."

Implied was the suggestion that he wasn't sorry for his reasoning.

Vivi rolled her eyes at him. She should have known better. After downing half her glass of water, she turned to tell him their interaction was over for now.

She really shouldn't be sparring with him—she should be resting her voice instead. The band was due to start in ten short minutes. She was on twenty minutes after that.

Whatever his issue was, she was going to have to deal with it later.

"I hope you enjoy your evening, Mr. Manning. I have a show to do." With that, she turned and walked away to the steps that led to the lower deck to start to get ready.

Maybe she was putting off the inevitable, but there wasn't any other choice right now. Whatever Zeke Manning wanted with her it was going to have to wait.

She was really something, all right. Zeke had no doubt about it as he watched Vivi's back as she left the bar area. He couldn't help but notice the other appreciative male gazes that followed her exit. She wasn't quite sashaying, but her movements somehow screamed out her allure and sex appeal. Long, shapely legs leading to a rounded, luscious bottom. Her waist was cinched by a thin gold chain that served as a threadlike belt around her silky black dress.

He squeezed his eyes shut. He really had no business looking at her dress or her curves.

Tomas was still glaring at him from the other side of the bar. Zeke held up his hands in mock surrender. He hadn't really done anything wrong. For all he knew, Vivi had indeed taken advantage of Esther when she was most vulnerable. Zeke just hadn't handled his suspicions well. But, truth be told, even their brief interactions had sewn a seed of doubt about her guilt. Not to mention, she certainly had a loyal friend in the bartender. Women who took advantage of little old ladies didn't usually inspire that kind of loyalty, did they?

He let out a disgusted grunt. What kind of question was that? He, of all people, knew how some individuals were charismatic and duplicitous enough to attract lost souls. Souls like his mother.

Still, Vivi didn't strike him as anyone who resembled his "uncle." Quote, unquote. Even calling the man by that title sent a surge of bile rising up in Zeke's throat. The ever-present memories dancing on the edge of his mind threatened to trot to the center before he squashed them back down. He dragged himself back to the present.

Tomas was clearly done serving him any more cocktails. He hadn't so much as acknowledged Zeke's existence since Vivienne had walked off, other than to send a withering glare in his direction. Shame. He could have used another glass of the punch. Just as well, he needed his wits about him when they finally had the conversation about Esther and the missing necklace. He hoped she had a good explanation. In fact, he wanted that to be true more than he would have imagined when he first boarded the boat. Which made absolutely no sense. That one scenario would be the fastest way to be done with the whole mess and get back to all the pressing matters waiting for him at the firm. He still had that trip to France coming up in a few short days. All the documents needed for the winery acquisition still needed to be drawn up and finalized. He really had no business drifting on a steamship on the Mississippi.

With a sigh, he pulled out his wallet and left a generous tip for the man who apparently didn't think him worthy of another minute of his time. He could hear the band starting up one deck below. The programs on the back of the plastic-coated menus indicated Vivienne wouldn't be onstage until after they played for a little while as dinner was served.

Well, he'd paid for said dinner. So he might as well eat.

A wall of aroma greeted him when he opened the double-wide door that led to the main ballroom. Buffet tables were set up in a half rectangle on the opposite side. Steam wafted from shiny silver trays. The band was between numbers, but struck up the first chord to the next song as Zeke shut the door behind him. A bouncy jazz number started to play with a trumpet blaring to accompany the rapid notes of the banjo. A drummer accentuated the rhythmic beat, and a piano player rounded out the foursome. Just like by the bar, Zeke didn't know anyone. And there'd be no bartender with a friendly smile to help keep him company. Not that that had lasted long.

At least the food looked good. In fact, between the scents of seafood, rice and gumbo, and the colorful array of salads and fruit, Zeke's mouth started to water.

Striding over to the buffet area, he grabbed a plate and stepped forward to the start of the line. He couldn't remember the last time he'd eaten buffet-style. This trip was turning into one big slew of surprises.

The touchy-feely couple he'd seen earlier was right in front of him. The man had one hand gripping a plate as he waited his turn, and the other wrapped around his lady's waist. She stood leaning tight against his side. Every few seconds, they faced each other for a quick yet ardent kiss on the lips.

What would that be like? Zeke had to wonder, making sure not to stare. To be that enamored of someone. Not the way his mother had been with Rex—that wasn't healthy or natural. That had been the type of relationship that ruined lives. No, there'd been nothing affectionate about that relationship. Just his mother's rampant gullibility and blatant disregard for all those who had the misfortune of depending on her.

Zeke made himself turn away from the couple and concentrated on filling his plate. Before he knew it, he was back up for seconds. The food was good—really good. The band was entertaining, and he couldn't deny that he was enjoying himself. He was debating going back for yet another helping when the lights in the room dimmed slightly. The band played out of the latest song and its members shifted to make more room in the center.

A moment later, Zeke found himself grateful that he hadn't gone up for more food. He didn't think he could swallow anything down. Vivienne stepped onto the stage and though she was wearing the same dress, her entire look had somehow morphed into something even sexier. She'd taken off the flat checkered Chucks and donned stilettos. Her hair was piled on top of her head. Scarlet red lipstick covered her mouth. That had to be the sexiest shade of red he'd ever seen.

Zeke shifted in his seat to somehow quell the

unwelcome surge of desire storming thorough his core. This wouldn't do. It had to be the novelty of the atmosphere. The fact that he was on a boat surrounded by arduous couples. Once he left New Orleans, and the business with the necklace was resolved, he would forget any kind of attraction he was feeling at the moment for Ms. Ducarne. He was convinced. But then she began to sing.

CHAPTER THREE

SHE'D NEVER HAD this much trouble concentrating on her performance. How many notes had she missed already? And the song she was performing was one she knew in her heart. It was her warm-up song, for heaven's sake. There was no excuse for messing up the way she was.

She knew exactly whom to blame.

Vivi tried to keep her gaze roaming around the entire audience and not on one individual in particular. The man who just happened to be sitting at one of the tables closest to the stage. He hadn't seemed to have taken his eyes off her. Which was disconcerting to say the least. Not that it should have been. She was onstage, after all. It was just that the way he was looking at her was making her think all sorts of wayward thoughts. Thoughts like how the dark hue of his eyes seemed even more dramatic in the dimly lit ballroom. And of the way she'd noticed his scent when she'd been sitting next to him at the bar. Like spearmint mixed with some kind of woodsy, rich scent she'd be hard-pressed to name. How his dark hair fell haphazardly across his forehead and had her fingertips itching with the desire to gently swipe the strands off his face.

She'd just sung off-key again. The audience seemed too distracted to notice, or maybe they didn't care, given all the food and drink distracting them. But both the drummer and piano player were giving her quizzical looks from under the brims of their straw hats.

Vivi somehow managed to finish the set without slipping up too badly. But her lackluster performance had her feeling out of sorts to say the least.

Enough was enough. After taking a bow to the applauding audience, she made a beeline to where Zeke Manning was still sitting at the same table.

"Why are you still here?"

He didn't so much as blink in reaction. "What? You were hoping Tomas might have thrown me overboard perhaps?"

"The thought is not without appeal."

"Sorry. No such luck." He pushed out a chair with his leg, motioned for her to sit down. "Why don't you join me?"

"You know what? I think I will." It was high time they had a little chat about what it was, exactly, that had Zeke Manning's knickers all twisted. Whatever it was, Vivi just knew she wasn't going to like it. Nothing like ripping the bandage right off. Ignoring the chair he'd kicked out for her, she pulled out the one farthest from him and sat. Though only a matter of inches, the petty gesture gave a small manner of satisfaction.

"Why exactly are you here, Mr. Manning?" she began without any preamble. "What is it that you want with me?"

She thought she saw a flicker of something pass behind his eyes. Probably just a trick of the light. Right now, all she wanted was some answers.

"I'm an estate attorney who specializes in appraisals."

"And?"

"And I'm here in New Orleans as a favor to my grandmother."

It was her turn to blink in confusion. Zeke wouldn't have struck her as the type who did favors for their grandmothers. "Come again?"

He nodded. "She's a friend of Esther Truneau."

"The sweet lady I do weekly readings for?"

"That's the one. You do the readings at her mansion, I was told."

Alarm bells started to ring in Vivi's head. "That's right. She used to come to the shop at first, but at her age, I offered to go to her instead. She's not terribly mobile, if you hadn't noticed."

Zeke casually rubbed his jaw, drawing her attention to the dark stubble of his five-o'clock shadow. The facial hair added another layer of edginess to his already jagged aura. "Hmm" was all he said in response.

Vivi really didn't like the way he said it. "What exactly does that mean?"

Zeke gave a small shrug. "I'm just curious. Do many fortune-tellers make house calls?"

Vivi crossed her arms in front of her chest. "First of all, I'm not a fortune-teller. I read tarot cards."

He waved that off with dismissal. "Six of one…"

She didn't bother to explain how wrong he was. Zeke made it sound as if she sat in a darkened tent at the traveling carnival with a crystal ball between her and a lovestruck teenager. Not that there was anything wrong with that. But Vivi had spent years studying the tarot. She took care to interpret and explain what she thought the cards meant in such a way as to make a real impact on her clients and how they lived their lives.

He motioned to the stage. "And obviously that's not all you do to earn a living."

The way he said the last three words sounded downright condescending. Of course he looked down at her. Everything about this man screamed prestigious attorney for the rich and powerful. He was clearly no ambulance chaser like the ones advertising on daytime television every afternoon who promised to "win you your due without even having to go to court!"

"I'm sure you've heard of the new gig economy in the US these days. Now, what's all this got to do with you being here in the city and following me to said gigs twice in one day?"

He leaned over the table, his elbows on the wrinkled paper mat. "Esther mentioned she's sometimes gifted you various items."

The alarm bells suddenly increased in both frequency and volume. "That's true. She told me she's ready to downsize and wants to get rid of some odds and ends."

He grunted out a laugh, but darned if she was in on the joke. "I believe she recently gave you a necklace."

Vivi nodded. "That's right. She said the red stones would go well with my dark hair."

Zeke quirked an eyebrow at her. "Those stones happen to be red rubies. On a platinum chain."

Vivi's mouth went dry. "Wait. Real rubies? On a real platinum chain?"

"That's right. The piece happens to be an

antique crafted in the eighteenth century in France."

Vivi swallowed past the heavy lump that had formed in her throat. "Are you telling me that wasn't costume jewelry? I—I thought it was a trinket, just a small token of Esther's appreciation."

Zeke leaned closer to her over the table. Vivi resisted the urge to draw back or to drop her gaze. She knew she had to meet this man eye-to-eye. Still, it was hard not to show any kind of reaction at his next words.

"It just so happens that the small trinket Esther gave you is highly valuable, and would probably fetch high six figures at auction."

She was good. Zeke had to give her that much. She'd barely reacted when he'd told her the estimated value of the item she'd so casually referred to as a "trinket." Still, he hadn't missed the near imperceptible flinch when he'd mentioned the actual sum.

Either Vivienne Ducarne was an actress of Oscar-worthy caliber or he really had shocked her with the revelation.

Now she sat across from him with her mouth agape, seemingly at a loss for words.

"Is this someone's idea of a sick joke?" she demanded finally after several silent seconds.

He shook his head in answer. "No joke. You have in your possession an extremely valuable piece, which should fetch close to a million dollars at any international auction."

She squeezed her eyes shut tight, took a deep breath. "But why would Esther give me something so valuable?"

Did she really have to ask? It was clear Vivienne was a bright, intelligent young woman. Clearly, she had to see what was happening to Esther right in front of her eyes.

Vivienne had to have noticed that Esther wasn't always speaking sensibly or remembering things. Just today, Zeke had noticed all the times she hadn't been quite lucid. "Because she's gradually losing her faculties. It might be the onset of dementia of some sort." He couldn't try and guess, since he was no medically trained professional. But even a layman could see what was obvious.

"Poor Esther," Vivienne said simply. Suddenly, her eyes grew wide. "Wait. You don't think I somehow tricked her to give me something that priceless. I didn't even know! How could I?" She clasped a hand to her mouth in horror. "Oh, my God! You threatened in the shop to come back with the authorities. You were ready to accuse me of theft, weren't you?"

She leaned closer to him over the table. "Valuable or not, I was given that necklace!"

Zeke ducked his head—she had him there. The threat *had* been a bit much coming from him before he'd so much as gathered any facts. "Yeah, look. About that."

Her palm remained on her mouth—he had her full attention. "I admit I may have been a bit…overzealous back there earlier today."

"Oh, you think?" she asked, her voice dripping with sarcasm. "You didn't even bother to explain or ask me my side of the story."

Zeke cleared his throat—she was right. He should have done more asking and less threatening. "I admit it. I didn't handle that very well."

She tilted her head, studying him. "You're not very good at apologizing, are you?"

An apology wasn't quite what he'd intended when he boarded the steamship, but he didn't bother to correct the assumption she'd jumped to. Again, he had to wonder if she was a gifted actress or really did consider herself to be the slighted party. Maybe it was both.

"I'm guessing you haven't had much practice apologizing to people," she added.

He had to laugh at that. She had no idea. He'd been made to apologize so often as a child. For even the smallest of slights. "I'm sorry for the way I behaved when we first met. Maybe we can do that part over."

Her eyes narrowed on him. "How do you propose we do that? You were ready to throw me to the wolves because you thought I was low enough to take advantage of a vulnerable old lady. You didn't even ask if I was innocent."

Not many guilty folks would actually admit it. Zeke kept that thought to himself. He wasn't quite ready to accept her total innocence. But he could give her the benefit of the doubt. He'd humor her until he learned more, at least. For now.

"How about we try to start over?" He stuck his hand out. "Hello. I'm Ezekiel Manning. Everyone calls me Zeke."

She looked at his outstretched hand with clear wariness, but made no move to take it for several moments. Finally, she took the end of his fingertips in a quick shake before pulling away. "I'm Vivienne Ducarne. As you know. Everyone calls me Vivi. And I did not knowingly take a priceless necklace."

"Nice to meet you, Vivi. Please just tell me it's in a safe place."

She nodded. "Yes. It's at my apartment. I gave it to my roommate because she admired it so much when I brought it home."

A surge of panic shot through Zeke's core. "You did what?"

"Don't worry. She wouldn't be wearing it tonight. She's waitressing the night shift at the Crawdad Café. No need for even costume jewelry there. We get covered from head to toe in powdered sugar and coffee syrup before our shifts ends."

"We? Our? You have yet another job, then?"

"This is a very expensive city, Mr. Manning. It takes a lot simply to make ends meet." Her voice was full of emotion and grievance as she said the words. He'd wounded her pride.

Great. Yet another slight he would have to find a way and time to apologize for. If he ever got the chance, he might have to explain to Ms. Ducarne just how little he came from. Though he went through extreme pains to make sure to hide it.

Vivienne changed the subject. "I'm sure it's on her dresser bureau, where she keeps her baubles."

Zeke had to suppress a shudder at the thought of such a priceless antique sitting among a slew of discount-store knickknacks. All that mattered was he'd discovered the location of the necklace. At least the mystery was over.

Vivi continued, "As soon as we dock, I'll head straight back to my place. I'll leave Bessa a text to tell her why I had to take it back. She's not going to believe this!"

Zeke could hardly blame her.

"We can get it back to Esther tonight," Vivi continued. "I have no desire to have anything that valuable in my possession a moment longer."

They took a cab from the Toulouse Street wharf to Vivi's neighborhood. Zeke studied the buildings they passed as the taxi came to a stop in front of her residence. Nestled between a restaurant and a candle shop, her house looked like something out of a children's storybook. A porch with hanging spider plants, pink-and-white shutters and two matching rocking chairs. The siding was a bright powder blue. The street held an eclectic mix of businesses and residential houses.

"Wait for me here," Vivi ordered as they exited the car and reached the sidewalk. "I'll be right down with it."

It was past eleven o'clock, yet the street bustled with activity. Different types of music poured out of every open window. A For Sale sign hung off a pole in front of the house across the street. A smaller sign in the window read Haunted in bright red letters. Interesting disclosure. Quite the selling point.

A group of teenagers walked by him, laughing and talking loudly. One of them sported a thick yellow boa wrapped around his neck. Zeke did a double take upon closer inspection. It was moving. The boa wasn't a decorative accessory, after all. Rather, it was a very large python. Vivi must have noticed his reaction to the reptile as she pulled her house key out of her purse.

"That's Nessie," she called back to him. "You can pet him if you'd like. I'm sure Tim will let you."

Zeke hoped his shiver wasn't terribly obvious. "No, thanks. I'll pass."

Vivi laughed, unlocking her door and pushing it open. It occurred to him that this was the first time he'd heard her laugh. Hearty yet soft. It sounded almost melodic...

He gave himself a mental smack. What in the world was wrong with him? Waxing poetic about the way a woman laughed?

The sooner this night was over with and the sooner he got the necklace back to its rightful owner, the sooner he could get back to normal.

He was unable to recognize this version of himself. Overindulging at a buffet, boarding steamships on a whim, noticing the sway of a woman's gait when she walked. The sound she made when she laughed.

Practically swooning while watching her sing onstage. He was acting like some hormonal teenager.

When was the last time he'd dated? It had been too long apparently. Maybe that was the problem. He'd been so busy with the firm and his growing clientele, not to mention his investment portfolio. He needed to get out more, as his ex, Marnie, had so loudly pointed out after he'd turned her down for yet another red-carpet event. Right before she'd stormed out of his apartment, cursing at him over her shoulder. He'd thought about calling her to apologize, but figured it was best they go their separate ways. An up-and-coming actress needed more time and effort than Zeke was ready to give.

A light came on upstairs on the second floor. Zeke glanced at his watch. Hopefully, this wouldn't take long. It was already too late to wake Esther, but he could at least get the necklace back to the Truneau estate sometime tonight. He'd sleep well knowing it was back where it belonged.

And what of Vivi?

The question nagged at him because it wasn't one he had any business asking. Twenty-four hours ago, he hadn't even known the woman existed. He had the firm's investigator looking into her and if the vetting proved unsatisfactory in any way, if anything unscrupulous turned up in her past, Zeke would make sure Esther knew and was protected. Other than that, after tonight, there was no reason to think about Vivienne Ducarne, let alone ever see her again.

A coil of displeasure tightened in his gut. What might have transpired between them under different circumstances? he wondered. They belonged in such different worlds. It was a wonder their paths had crossed at all. If he had happened to run into her during one of his business trips to Louisiana, would he even have noticed her?

Something told him the opposite was definitely not likely. A free spirit like Vivi would probably not look twice at a businessman like himself. The guys she dated were probably all as eclectic as she was.

They really had nothing in common. And their first encounter had been less than cordial. Still, imagining running into her at a different time and in a different place brought all sorts of intriguing pictures to his imagination.

The taxi driver rolled down his window, interrupting Zeke's musings.

"How much longer, man? I got calls coming in from dispatch."

Zeke glanced at his watch. How long had it been? More than the couple of minutes it should have taken for her to retrieve the necklace, then head back down. Even accounting for a potential run to her restroom, or a quick stop in the kitchen, Vivi should have come back by now.

"I'm sure she'll be down in no time," he answered the cabbie, somehow managing to keep the uncertainty out of his voice.

But several more minutes passed. A curl of unease ran down his spine. She definitely should have been down by now. Possibilities he didn't want to explore tried invading his mind. Had he been duped? Was he standing here like an idiot on the sidewalk because she had no intention of coming back down? Maybe she'd even cut and run using a back door.

That made no sense. She clearly lived here—she'd entered with a key. Why would she bring him to her home only to try and ditch him when he could come back to find her at any time?

There was one way to find out.

He was about to run up the steps to ring her doorbell when she finally reappeared. Even in the dim glow of the porch tea lights, he could tell by her pallor that something was terribly wrong. She was pale as a sheet. The unease he'd been feeling turned into full-blown trepidation as she spoke.

"It's not here."

CHAPTER FOUR

ZEKE DIDN'T EVEN know why he was surprised. Why had he expected things to go without a hitch in the first place? Nothing that had happened since he'd first laid eyes on Vivienne Ducarne should have ever given him the impression that things would run smoothly where she was concerned.

"Are you sure?" he asked her, though he was certain of the answer.

She nodded briskly, her head bobbing up and down. "Positive. I looked everywhere. Pretty much tore the apartment upside down. Esther's necklace is nowhere to be found. It's gone."

In a colossal case of bad timing, the cabbie bleeped his car horn twice. What was wrong with the man? The meter was running, after all. Zeke held his hands up, asking him to wait.

"What about your roommate? Maybe she is indeed wearing it. Have you tried calling her?"

Vivi glared at him in response to his question. "Of course. What do you take me for?"

Zeke threw his hands up in frustration. "And? What did she say? Does she have it?"

"Don't you think I would have told you if I had an answer to that?" she demanded. "She didn't answer her phone. I didn't really expect her to. We're not allowed to carry our phones on the dining floor when we're serving. And I know she would have taken her only break by now."

Zeke pinched the bridge of his nose. "You could have led with that information when I asked about your roommate."

The cabbie interrupted yet again. Rolling down his window, he leaned his head out to yell at them. "Listen, man. Y'all ain't paying me enough to just sit here idle."

Zeke walked over to the open window and handed the man several bills as a tip to add to the meter reading. But without waiting any longer, as soon as he took the cash, the cabbie rolled the car forward and drove off. None too slowly.

Zeke swore under his breath. "Great. Now we have to find another ride." He rounded on Vivi, a little more abruptly than he'd meant to. "How could this have happened?"

She didn't so much as flinch. Rather, her chin jutted upward. "Our driver got tired of waiting for us and he left."

Zeke sucked in a deep breath, aiming for some semblance of calm. If she was trying to aggravate him, it was working. "You know very well our loss of transportation is not what I'm referring to. How could the necklace not be where you were certain it would be?"

Clearly, giving Vivienne Ducarne the benefit of the doubt had been a mistake. Zeke wanted to kick himself for playing the fool. Was she playing some kind of game with him, trying to dupe him somehow? But if that was the case, why would she have brought him to her house in the first place?

Curiosity mingled with irritation and churned in his core. Maybe she was lying about where she thought the necklace would be. But he'd play along for now. In for a penny and all that.

"Don't snap at me," she growled. "That's not exactly helping matters. We just need to talk to Bessa. Ask where she's put it." She pulled her bangs off her forehead. "I wish I'd never laid eyes on the confounded thing."

"How can we ask this Bessa anything if she's not answering her phone?" Zeke asked.

She puffed out a breath before answering. "Let's just go to the café. Talk to her directly. Her shift doesn't end for another two hours."

Zeke pulled his phone out of his pocket,

swearing once more, this time at the disloyal and impatient cab driver. "I'll call for another car."

She touched him on the wrist before he could dial. A strange current seemed to travel over his skin where her hand made contact. And wasn't this a fine time to be noticing such a thing.

"Don't bother. It's just as easy to walk. It's just through the main square."

She dropped her hand and turned on her heel. "Be forewarned, though."

Warned? What fresh peril awaited them now? "About what?" he asked, following in her path.

"The French Quarter is a chaotic party zoo this time of night."

Despite the more pressing matters they were dealing with at the moment, her statement struck Zeke as rather odd. "Why do you feel the need to warn me about that?"

She shrugged. "Something tells me you're not exactly the outdoor, citywide-partying type."

She had no idea how loaded her comment was. Zeke didn't bother to try and elaborate. Vivi was right. He didn't like crowds. He didn't like chaos. Another reason why Marnie had broken up with him. He'd worked hard all his life for order and structure and discipline. Because he'd been exposed to too much of the opposite in his younger years. If they'd met under different circumstances, he might very well have told

Vivi about all the ways his childhood could have been a disturbing movie. But tonight wasn't the night. And it made no sense to rehash any of his past, anyway. That's exactly where he'd put it all—squarely in his past.

She wasn't kidding about the rowdiness. As they approached the cross street, the level of noise grew gradually louder and the handful of people out and about slowly grew to parade-size crowd numbers.

Vivi must have sensed his thoughts. "You should see it at Mardi Gras. This is nothing."

"How do you know I've never been to New Orleans for Mardi Gras?"

A small smile danced at the corners of her mouth. "Again. You don't seem the type."

"You're making quite a few assumptions about me, Ms. Ducarne. Might I remind you that we just met?" Little did she know, he'd grown up with quite the partiers.

"Well, that's rich," she replied as they passed a juggler entertaining a small crowd. The tall thin man in a tracksuit tossed several sharp objects in the air and caught them effortlessly to the sounds of oohs and aahs from those watching him.

"What's that?"

"Considering how you made a major assumption about me before you'd even met me."

Zeke sighed slowly. "Yes, we've already established I was being a—"

She supplied a noun that didn't bear repeating. "And it was more than that," she countered. "You accused me of being a thief."

So she still held a grudge about that first meeting. Zeke didn't bother to voice his thoughts aloud—for someone who still hadn't produced the necklace, Vivi certainly played the part of the injured party very well.

They didn't bother to speak the rest of the way. It would have been near impossible to hear over the noise that surrounded them as they walked through the massive crowds.

Finally, Vivi turned a corner, passing a group of tap dancers using flattened soda cans as makeshift tap shoes. Half a crowded block later, they approached a glass-walled diner-style café with open-air seating. Every table was full, the hum of conversations accompanying a single pianist on the stage in the corner. The man's fingers moved furiously over the keys as he played a fast-paced jazz number that sounded vaguely familiar to Zeke's ears. He finally recognized the tune as an instrumental version of a popular hip-hop song. Two couples were dancing a complicated number between the tables.

One thing about New Orleans—the music

and dancing never seemed to stop. Vivi spotted a group leaving their chairs and immediately nabbed the table. The woman sure could move fast when she needed to.

"This isn't her section, but we can try and steal her away," she explained as Zeke pulled out his own chair to sit. The sweet scent of sugar and fried dough wafted in the air. His taste buds reacted in response. He didn't possess much of a sweet tooth, but the smell of freshly fried beignets was hard to ignore.

"You want something to eat or drink?" she asked, somewhat surprising him. "The beignets are as good as they smell." She really was rather intuitive. Maybe it had something to do with her fortune-telling. He'd have to remind himself not to refer to that particular job that way if it came up again. She hadn't liked that description.

He shook his head in answer. "Maybe later. Let's just find your roommate and be on with it."

"There she is," Vivi suddenly exclaimed and jumped up. "Bessa! Over here!"

The other woman smiled immediately as soon as she spotted where Vivi was standing. She was over by their side in less than half a dozen strides.

"Hey, sugar!" Bessa yelled over the noise, then clutched Vivi in a tight embrace as if they hadn't seen each other in weeks. "Whatcha doin' here?" Bessa asked when she finally let Vivi go. Her gaze darted in Zeke's direction. "And who is this fine-looking gentleman you've brought with you?"

Zeke stood to introduce himself. "Zeke Manning. I'm here from Manhattan on business." He held out his hand, but Bessa surprised him when she ignored it. Instead, she stepped closer, grabbing him in the same bear hug she'd just released Vivi from and squeezing him tight. "Uh, nice to meet you," Zeke said over the woman's shoulder right before she let him go. "As for why we're here…" He motioned over to Vivi to take over and explain.

"Bessa, I know it's super busy here," Vivi began. "But can you spare a moment? It's important."

Bessa glanced around to the other side of the café, then over to the bar area. "The barista is shorthanded and way behind. So I've got a minute or two until she puts out my table's orders. What's going on?" Immediate concern flushed over her features as she studied Vivi's agitated state. "Everything all right? You look like you've been caught doing something you shouldn't have been doing." She gave Zeke a loaded look, adding a mischievous smile.

Zeke grunted out an unamused laugh. She had no idea how accurate her description was.

"If you only knew," Vivi answered.

Bessa pulled out a chair and all three of them sat. "Tell me."

Vivi quickly explained the situation, luckily leaving out the part where Zeke had confronted her in the magic shop before it all began. There was clearly a lot of affection between the two women and he didn't feel like landing on the roommate's bad side so soon upon meeting. He recalled Tomas's earlier visual warning at the steamship bar.

Vivi certainly seemed to be emotionally close to the people in her life. Now Bessa's eyes grew wide as she listened to her explain the events of the past twelve hours. When she was done, the other woman was completely still, her mouth agape.

"It's true," Vivi emphasized. "The necklace is worth a ton of money. We have to get it back to Ms. Truneau."

Bessa seemed at a loss for words. "Oh, my," she finally said, somewhat hesitantly.

"I had no idea it was so valuable," Vivi repeated for what had to be the tenth time.

"Now, why would that ol' lady just hand you something like that? Like it was nothing more than a carnival bead chain or something?" Bessa asked.

Zeke decided to step in. "She's not quite herself lately," he said vaguely. "What matters is we return her property."

Vivi nodded with solemn agreement. "As much as I hate to reclaim a gift I gave you, it can't be helped. I'll make it up to you, Bessa."

"Girl." Bessa slammed her palms on her hips, seemingly offended. "That's not it. You know I wouldn't ever hold you to something like that."

"Then what is it? Can you tell me where the necklace is?"

Bessa's eyebrows drew together and she clasped her hands in front of her powdered-sugar-covered apron.

For the second time in under an hour, a feeling of low dread washed through Zeke's chest. He didn't have any idea what Bessa was about to tell them. But he was certain she wasn't about to say the exact location of Esther's antique necklace.

It appeared their journey wasn't quite over yet.

Vivi really just wanted this all to be over. But everything about Bessa's expression and demeanor told her she was about to deliver some really bad news. Bessa confirmed that suspicion as soon as she spoke again.

"Listen, sugar. I don't know how to tell you this…"

Vivi resisted the urge to stick her fingers in

her ears like a petulant toddler who didn't want to hear a reprimand. She could just guess what was coming. "I no longer have the necklace," Bessa informed them.

Bingo.

In the chair next to her, Zeke wearily rubbed his forehead. He didn't seem particularly surprised at the latest turn of events.

"What do you mean you don't have it?" Vivi asked past the lump in her throat.

Bessa leaned closer to her over the table. "Well, you know how Roxie's getting married, right?"

Vivi nodded absentmindedly, though she was decidedly confused. What did any of this have to do with Roxie's impending nuptials to the mechanic she'd met two months ago, when he'd towed her car after it had broken down on Canal Street?

"Who is Roxie?" Zeke asked. As if that really made any kind of difference in the overall scheme of things.

"She's one of the other servers here," Bessa answered. "Really sweet girl. Plans on eloping with her beau, whom she met a few weeks back. I hope the marriage lasts—I do. She deserves some happiness."

Vivi cleared her throat to interrupt the tangent. Zeke was looking at both of them with utter bewilderment on his face. "Perhaps you could tell us what Roxie has to do with this," Vivi said.

Bessa visibly cringed as she answered. "Well, it's like you said. Just like you, I had no idea how valuable this piece of jewelry was. And Roxie's about to get married. Even though the happy couple plans to elope, it's still only proper to give them a wedding gift, right?"

Vivi's blood turned to ice in her veins. *Oh, no.* This couldn't be happening.

"Let me guess," Zeke began, pinching the bridge of his nose. "You gave said piece of jewelry to the bride-to-be."

Bessa nodded slowly. "I'm afraid so."

Zeke swore elaborately next to her. A rather descriptive curse that involved sharp objects and places that saw no sunlight. Honestly, the man spoke like a sailor on leave. She'd grown up in New Orleans and had heard more than her fair share of colorful language. But coming from someone as sophisticated and polished as he appeared to be, it was just a tad jarring.

Not that she could blame him in this particular instance.

Bessa grabbed her hand over the table in reassurance. "But don't worry. They haven't left yet. I'll just sneak my phone and go call her to explain what's happened. Tell her she needs to give the necklace back." She gave Vivi's hand a squeeze. "You two just wait here and relax."

Easier said than done, Vivi thought as she watched her friend walk away. "Do you want a beignet while we wait?" Vivi asked, more for something to say than any kind of attempt at hospitality. "My treat. It's on the house. Employee perk."

"Sure. Why not?"

Vivi raised her arm and the section's server appeared at their table within moments. The woman was a relatively new hire, and Vivi didn't know her well, but she seemed nice enough. "What can I get y'all?" she asked in a thick Creole accent.

Vivi ordered beignets and coffee for both of them. Though rather late to be drinking coffee, Vivi had a hunch they were going to be up for a while longer and needed the boost. It was relatively early by NOLA standards, but she felt like this day had lasted a fortnight already.

Bessa still hadn't returned by the time their food arrived. In between giving her looks of consternation, Zeke kept glancing at his watch. To his credit, he hadn't made any cutting remarks yet about their lack of success in retrieving Esther's necklace.

Neither of them touched the beignets, though he downed about half the strong chicory roast within moments of it being placed in front of him. Vivi guessed he probably wasn't really tasting it. He probably wanted this night to be done with as much as she did.

Simply to give herself something to do, Vivi reached for a beignet and took a small bite. She nearly moaned in delight despite herself. Jess was at the fryer tonight. The man somehow made magic with dough and hot oil.

Zeke lifted both eyebrows at her reaction. "That good, huh?"

She swallowed, savoring the sweet concoction melting on her tongue. "You have to try one to believe how good they are."

Giving a small shrug, Zeke reached for one of the pastries. His eyes grew wide when he took a bite.

"Wow."

Vivi couldn't help the bubble of laughter that escaped her lips. The expression on his face reminded her of a toddler who'd just had his first taste of ice cream. Or a someone from New York who'd just bit into his first authentic Louisiana beignet.

Through her chuckle, she took another bite of her own treat. Zeke had his finished in two quick bites. "Please, have the other two," she insisted. "I have these daily."

"Don't mind if I do," he replied, but stopped

in the act of reaching for another. His eyes narrowed on her face.

Oh, Lord. Vivi knew what he had to be staring at. She no doubt had powdered sugar all over her face. She'd been eating these things her whole life, worked in a café that employed a man who specialized in making them to perfection and she still hadn't learned to consume them without making a complete mess.

In horrified embarrassment, she reached for the napkin dispenser and pulled out more than a few, then hurriedly began trying to clean herself up.

"You missed a bit," Zeke told her, and before she could react, his hand reached out and rubbed a spot right above her lip. The touch of his warm fingers so near her mouth sent a strange sensation through her center. Despite the heavy scent of sugar and hot oil, she could still smell the woodsy mint hint of his aftershave. He'd undone the top two buttons of his shirt sometime over the evening, revealing a tan vee of skin. Was it her imagination, or had his hand lingered near her mouth a scant second longer than it had to?

Time seemed to stand still and neither of them moved. Finally, Zeke dropped his arm.

What had just happened? Sure, Zeke happened to be a very attractive man. But she couldn't be attracted to him. He lived in Manhattan. He was a high-powered attorney who clearly did very well for himself. While she had three undependable jobs.

Her roommate chose that moment to reappear at the table. Vivi dropped the bunched-up napkins on the table and stood.

"Bessa, what did Roxie say? Can we get the necklace from her tonight?"

Bessa rubbed a palm down her face. "I'm sorry, sugar. I'm afraid I have more bad news."

CHAPTER FIVE

ZEKE FIGURED HE must have misheard what Bessa had just said. "If you want that necklace, you're gonna have to go to Niagara Falls."

He could only repeat the last two words, dumbfounded. "Niagara Falls?"

Bessa nodded. "Yeah. But don't worry. It's the US side. You don't have to cross the border or anything."

Right, as if that had been Zeke's main concern at this latest, strange new turn of events.

Maybe Bessa was making complete sense and the problem was him. He wasn't processing correctly. His head still felt like it was spinning, after all. What had possessed him to reach out and touch Vivi the way he had just prior to Bess returning? He could have just as easily pointed out to her where to wipe the sugar off her mouth. But before he knew he'd intended to do it, his fingers were on her skin.

Heaven help him, he hadn't wanted to stop.

He'd wanted to linger on her face, then trail his fingers along her soft, feminine jawline. He wanted to taste that small speck of sugar right off her lips.

Zeke gave himself a mental shake. He had to stop the treacherous line of thought. None of it made any sense. For one, he'd only just met the woman. Oh, and there was also the small matter of a major antique having gone missing that he was somehow responsible for finding.

Speaking of said missing antique, Bessa was now saying something about a chapel. Right, the wedding of Roxie and her mechanic beau. It was hard to keep track of all the details. Especially considering how fast they were coming at him.

Vivi looked just as perplexed as he was. "But I thought they weren't due to leave until early tomorrow. And why are they in Niagara Falls? Don't people usually elope in Las Vegas?"

Bessa clapped her hands once in front of her chest. "See! That's what I thought. But it turns out there's plenty of twenty-four-hour chapels in Niagara Falls, New York. It is the honeymoon capital of the world, after all, you know."

"Huh," Vivi replied. "I didn't actually know that."

Zeke might have heard that fact once or twice. Simply because he made his life in Manhattan now. Though Niagara Falls was farther north. A hop and a skip from the Canadian border. Apparently, couples in a rush to get married found something romantic about gushing, loud waterfalls. The city served as an alternative to those who found Vegas too bawdy.

"Sure," Bessa said, breaking in to Zeke's thoughts. "Couples go there, get married, then start their honeymoon right away. Turns out that's what Roxie and Rocky decided to do. And they didn't want to wait until tomorrow."

Zeke knew he shouldn't even go there, but he couldn't seem to help himself. "Did you say Roxie is marrying someone named Rocky?"

Both women looked at him like they didn't understand the question. "Never mind." Yep, he should have known better.

"Anyway," Bessa continued, "Roxie's mom told me all that. It took me so long because I couldn't get a hold of Roxie herself. I had to track down her momma. She said the happy couple doesn't want to be disturbed during this special time, so they're probably not checking their phones. They haven't even sent the poor woman any photos of their vow taking. Can you believe that?"

"I find all of this pretty hard to believe," Zeke muttered under his breath.

"What was that?" Bessa asked.

"Nothing. Forget it."

She turned back to face Vivi. "I'm sorry about all this, hon. I'd have never given it to her if I'd known."

Vivi reached over and rubbed her roommate's upper arm. "It's not your fault, Bessa. I'm the one who should be apologizing."

Zeke found himself wanting to apologize as well. Though for the life of him he couldn't say why or what for. But it was hard not to feel as if part of this was somehow his fault, too.

Bessa squeezed Vivi's hand on her arm. "Well, I better get back to work. My tables are getting antsy and at least one café au lait is probably too cold by now."

Vivi nodded as the other woman walked away.

She turned to him finally, rubbing a hand down her face. "Now what do we do?"

If this was some kind of con or hoax, then Vivi would have to be the most talented hustler this side of the equator. There was no way anyone could have planned something so convoluted with so many people in such a short amount of time. As ridiculous as it was, there didn't seem to be anything nefarious going on. Esther's necklace had really somehow traveled all the way from New Orleans, Louisiana, to Niagara Falls, New York. He almost had to laugh.

Zeke weighed the possible options. He could hire somebody to go there, find this Roxie and

Rocky—his mind made a mental pause at the names yet again, despite himself—and somehow convince them to hand over a wedding gift that just happened to be priceless to a complete stranger.

He couldn't even count all the ways that scenario could go wrong.

Or he could take the chance of waiting for the honeymooners to return in a few days. That option ran the risk of the necklace getting lost or stolen through their travels. Or, heaven forbid, tossed like a carnival toy into the rushing waterfall. Though unlikely, anything was possible with giddy newlyweds. He remembered reading in some travel magazine that people threw all sorts of items into the falls on the superstition that it brought about good luck. A shudder ran down his spine at the image of Esther's priceless rubies and stones being pummeled by thousands of tons of water until they disintegrated into fine dust.

He released a resigned sigh before answering Vivi's question. "There doesn't seem to be much of a choice from where I'm standing."

Vivi slowly shook her head. "You can't mean what I think you're saying."

He shrugged. "You heard your friend as well as I did. If we want to get that necklace back to its rightful owner, we're going to have to go to Niagara Falls."

The look of consternation on her face matched his own. But they really did have no choice. By this time tomorrow night, they would have to be in Niagara Falls.

Vivi led Zeke out of the café at a loss for words. It had become almost comically complicated trying to get Esther's necklace back.

"We should probably talk about our exact game plan," Zeke said behind her as they stepped onto the sidewalk. "And I could use a drink. How about you?"

"I'm guessing you don't mean the caffeinated kind."

"You'd be guessing right."

Despite the late hour and the toll of the day's events, Vivi knew she wouldn't be able to get any sleep if she tried to go back home now, anyway. Plus, Zeke was right. They had some things to go over if they were to be traveling across the country sometime tomorrow. "I know just the place. Follow me."

A solo saxophonist played a sultry tune on the corner just past the café as Zeke paused to drop several bills into the man's open instrument case. Some teens were doing acrobatic stunts in the grassy area across the street to a rapt audience. Vivi led Zeke down past the park toward Canal Street. Finally, they turned down Bourbon, where the noise level ratcheted up several notches all at once. It was a pretty good crowd for this time on a weeknight.

"You seem to have a lot of competition out this way," Zeke commented, pointing to a neon sign above a shop door that said Tarot and Palm Readings. "How does one end up in that line of work, anyway?" he asked. Maybe she was being oversensitive, but she could swear she detected a note of derision in his voice at the question.

She cleared her throat, trying not to sound defensive as she answered. "One of my foster mothers was into it. She taught me about the cards."

Zeke's response could be described as a grunt.

Despite herself, Vivi paused in her tracks to try and explain what people like him were so unlikely to see. Zeke stopped and looked at her in question.

"It's about more than the cards, you know," she told him, not that he was likely to understand.

"I don't get it." Bingo, she was right.

"It's about the person you're reading for. Their fears, their anxieties. Things they want to get off their chest. Just to have someone safe to talk to."

His eyes flickered over her face. "Then I can see why you'd be good at that."

Vivi felt a warmth flush through her chest straight down to her toes. "That sounded suspiciously like it might be a compliment."

"You should take it as one."

His words sent a ridiculous giddiness through her.

Not trusting herself to respond without saying something embarrassingly cringey, she continued toward their destination. Several moments passed in awkward silence until Zeke finally cleared his throat and broke it with a question.

"We seem to have taken the long way to Bourbon. Any particular reason?"

"I just thought we could use the air," she answered with a shrug, though it was a bit of a fib. Just one more thing Zeke was unlikely to truly understand and would be too risky for her to tell him. She didn't want to explain why she'd gone out of her way to avoid walking past a certain pawnshop. The sight of the place still sent her pulse shooting sky-high and anxiety surging through her core. Zeke didn't need to know that it was where she'd found herself arrested and in handcuffs, the only thing she'd been guilty of being that she'd trusted the wrong man.

* * *

"New Orleans could definitely give New York City a run for its money as the city that never sleeps," Zeke commented as they made their way farther down Bourbon Street.

"I wouldn't know," Vivi answered. "I've never been there."

He was about to say that they would have to rectify that, that perhaps he could bring her to Manhattan one day and have her visit his penthouse apartment. But he stopped the words from leaving his mouth.

There was no sound reason for Vivienne Ducarne to visit him once this business with the necklace was over and done with. The notion sent a wave of strange emotion rushing through him, but he didn't want to explore why.

"That's too bad," he said simply instead.

They passed several smoky bars and taverns that looked like they served perfectly good spirits, but Vivi kept walking. Finally, they came upon a rather empty club that could aptly be described as a hole in the wall. Vivi walked through the open door and motioned for him to follow. The inside was dark and misty with walls painted blue and mirrored panels along the ceiling.

This was the place she had in mind?

He had to ask. "Not to question your judgment as a local, but why here?"

"Why not?"

"Well, we passed several other places that were much busier."

She led him to a table booth as she answered. "Like you said. I'm a local. Those other places are teeming with tourists who don't know where the best drinks, food and entertainment really are. Or where you don't have to wait several minutes just to put a drink order in."

That made sense. Zeke sat across from her on the vinyl-padded bench and a server immediately appeared as if to verify Vivi's statement about not having to wait.

"Hey, Vivi," the woman said as she smiled at them both in turn. "Your usual, I'm guessing. And what can I get for this fine specimen of a man you've brought in with you tonight?" She gave Zeke a not-too-subtle wink.

"I'll just have whatever she's having."

Vivi gave him a wide smile when he turned his attention back to her. "What?" he asked as the server went to get their drinks.

"I'm impressed. How spontaneous of you, to not even ask what my usual is before ordering it for yourself."

That was just it, wasn't it? He was acting very uncharacteristically today. Ever since he'd first laid eyes on Vivi, to be precise. Spontaneity wasn't a quality he was normally associated with. But so far he'd taken an unplanned cruise on a steamship, had followed Vivi to a dive bar in a hidden corner of Bourbon Street and was headed for an unexpected trip the next day.

"I'm not going to regret it, am I?" Zeke wasn't even sure if he was referring to the drink order or something else entirely.

He had part of the answer when the server reappeared with two goblets full of a red liquid accompanied by mini bottles of hot sauce.

"Two Cajun Cannons," the woman announced, placing everything on the table in front of them.

Vivi poured the hot sauce into the drink and took a small sip, and he followed suit. It was good. Surprisingly so. The spiciness hit just the right spot after all the sugar from the beignet earlier.

"So we're really doing this, huh?" Vivi asked after another sip of her drink. "Traveling to Niagara Falls."

He nodded. "I'll have a car pick you up tomorrow and take you to the jet at the airport."

She blinked at him. "The jet?"

"We'll be flying private. I'll have to have my pilot see about getting emergency clearance for a flight plan."

"Your pilot." She clasped her hands together over the table. "Am I to understand that we'll be heading to New York in your very own private jet?"

He could only nod again. Every once in a while, in moments such as this one, it occurred to Zeke just how much he took for granted in the life he'd managed to build for himself.

"How does one come about owning one's very own jet?" Vivi asked.

"I appraise some very valuable estates for some very knowledgeable people. Along the way I picked up a little bit about how to invest in valuables and other portfolios. It's all paid off rather well."

She blinked at him again, then took several gulps of her cocktail. "I see."

But she didn't. Vivi had no idea just how little he'd come from. Suddenly, he found himself wanting to explain it to her. But where would he start, exactly? "Things aren't always as they seem, Vivi."

To his surprise, she responded with a peal of giggles, then finally added, "Trust me, I'm not one who needs to hear that."

He had no doubt Vivi had a story that would likely match his own. Zeke hoped he might hear it someday. Maybe she didn't know exactly where to start, either.

A band began setting up on the small wooden stage in the corner. Soon, the sounds of bluesy jazz began to fill the air.

Vivi started to sway to the music in her seat. It was hard not to stare. She sat up straight. "You know what? I think we need to dance."

"Dance? Now?"

She was already standing as she answered. "Yep. You're being spontaneous, right?"

Without waiting for a response, she strode to the dance floor. What choice did he have but to follow her?

The cocktail must have been stronger than he thought. Because after the second or third number, Vivi was somehow in his arms as they moved to the music.

Zeke forgot about the circumstances that had led them to this moment. None of it mattered. Vivi felt right in his embrace, fit perfectly up against his length. They'd only just met, but everything about holding her felt familiar. Like she'd been in his arms his whole life, like she belonged there.

"You know, you're not such a bad dancer," she told him. "For an attorney," she added with a mischievous smile.

She was teasing him. For any outside observer, they might look like a couple out on a date. With a night full of possibilities ahead of them.

He really couldn't allow himself to think along those lines. "Thank you for the compliment. I guess us attorneys just need the right partner."

Vivi's gasp at his answer was almost imperceptible. But there was no mistaking the way her hands tightened where they were resting on his upper arms. Reflexively, he pulled her tighter against his chest. He could feel her warmth against his skin, smell the fruity scent of her shampoo. Her lips parted on a soft sigh and he had to wonder what those lips would taste like against his.

Heaven help him, he wanted to kiss her. But something told him there'd be no going back if he gave in to that temptation. So he would settle for simply holding her.

Zeke lost track of time as they moved together. His sole focus was on the woman he held in his arms.

He hardly noticed when the last song faded to a finish, because he didn't want this night to end. But Vivi stopped moving moments after the music ended. She slowly stepped out of his embrace. He felt her loss like a cold gust of wind.

"We should probably call it a night," she said, not quite meeting his eyes. "I'm guessing we have a long day ahead of us tomorrow."

She was right, of course. But Zeke found it hard to refrain from reaching for her again, and had to clench his fists to keep from doing so.

None of this made any kind of sense. Who would have thought when he'd met Vivienne Ducarne in the magic shop that he'd be slow dancing to jazz music with her in his arms less than twenty-four hours later?

Or how hard it would be for him to let her go?

This was so much more than she'd bargained for. What had possessed her to ask Zeke to dance with her last night?

And how in the world had she ended up here? Vivi could count on one hand all the times she'd flown on an airplane and still have a couple of digits left over. Now here she was, sitting on a private jet as it taxied down the runway at Louis Armstrong International Airport en route to Buffalo, New York, of all places. It was a city she'd only heard about on the news, watching reports of record snowfalls.

She'd tossed and turned all night with indecision, had reached for her phone countless times to call and tell Zeke that she couldn't go to Niagara Falls with him, after all. Slow dancing with him in a darkened club after having a strong cocktail had been a foolish and impulsive move. How much worse might it get if she was traveling with him across the country? But her conscience had won out in the end. The sad truth was, she felt more than a little guilty for Esther having lost such a valuable possession.

Also, there was the other much more pressing issue—if the necklace wasn't returned and the authorities became involved, that could cause a dangerous turn as far as she was concerned. Everything she'd worked so hard for, the peaceful and fulfilling life she'd managed to build for herself, could all be in jeopardy. Of course, she couldn't share any of that with Zeke. He would never understand and he'd probably jump to all the wrong conclusions without so much as listening to her end of the story. He might have been a charming and attentive partner last night on the dance floor, but Vivi knew how he would view her if he found out about her past. Like so many others in her life, Zeke would assume the worst.

Just like when he'd stormed into Lucien's Magic Shop and Gift Store.

In any case, it was much too late to be second-guessing things now, she figured as the airplane's tires ate up the runway and the aircraft accelerated before it began to lift off.

"I've taken the liberty of having some breakfast prepared and brought on board for us," Zeke said, interrupting her thoughts. "As soon as we reach a cruising altitude, the flight attendant will bring a few trays out. Along with hot coffee."

Vivi definitely could use the coffee given her restless night. All night long she'd wondered if agreeing to go with him on this trip was a wise decision. The man was so charming it was downright disconcerting. She thought about their time together the night before at the blues club. For such a straitlaced and conservative type, Zeke wasn't too bad a dancer. Color her surprised, but he'd thrown her off with his footwork. Being around him threw her off in ways she couldn't explain in general.

And if she needed any reminders that they came from two completely different worlds, the fact that she was traveling as his companion on his very own private jet certainly fit the bill.

"You look unsettled," Zeke said, studying her. "Are you a nervous flyer?"

"I'm not any kind of flyer," she admitted. "I've never actually left Louisiana. I have a passport but it's just for ID. And I certainly haven't flown private before."

Zeke ignored that last comment. "Maybe something to calm your nerves instead of coffee, then. A mimosa perhaps?"

Vivi shook her head. "No, thank you." How odd it was to be sitting here as Zeke offered her drinks and snacks. Usually, she was the one pouring coffee or mixing mimosas if she happened to be working a morning shift at the Crawdad Café. To have someone on standby somewhere in the cabin, waiting to serve her breakfast, seemed surreal.

It was certainly a far cry from the old days. She would have never guessed when she was a teen being bounced from one foster home to the next with nothing but the clothes on her back that she'd be in such a luxurious aircraft with a handsome businessman asking her what she desired.

A bubble of ironic laughter gurgled up her throat before she could suppress it. Not that she was forgetting how temporary all this was.

Suddenly, she felt completely out of place— underdressed and ill-prepared. She hadn't given much thought to clothing, just packed an overnight bag with toiletries and some extra unmentionables. A tank top with a cartoon crawfish under a light sweater seemed like a reasonable enough getup to travel in. Worn but comfortable Chucks rounded out her outfit.

Yep, downright peasant-like in comparison to her travel companion. Zeke was clad in pressed gray dress pants and a silk navy shirt that brought out the deep hue of his eyes. The laced leather shoes he wore were polished to a gleam and probably cost more than her entire wardrobe.

Despite what he'd said yesterday about giving her the benefit of the doubt, she knew someone like him would be way too quick to jump to believe the worst when it came to people like her.

"Will you be missed?" he asked, confusing her with the question before he clarified. "By your employers, I mean. I know this was a rather unexpected trip."

She shrugged. "Lucien just announced online that the tarot readings would have to be rescheduled. The new girl said she would take over my shift at the café and I'm not due to sing on the boat cruise until next week."

Zeke loosened his seat-belt buckle and leaned back in his seat. "I see. Is any of that going to set you back? We should be able to work something out. For all practical purposes, you're here traveling with me to assist with a job. As such, I'd be happy to compensate you for your time."

He may as well have struck her.

Vivi tried her best not to visibly bristle with offense. He was essentially looking at her as an employee of his. How right she'd been about the way he must see her. A working-class girl who could hardly afford to miss a shift here and there. Never mind that his assumption stung because it happened to be so close to the truth.

To think, she'd entertained the notion that they might be developing some kind of friendship last night. How silly of her. Zeke was a wealthy estate attorney who owned a private jet. He may not have said it out loud, but she knew he looked down upon her tarot-reading work. She knew he didn't see it as a legitimate way to earn money. Just because he'd told her she must be good at it, didn't mean he respected it.

Well, she was proud of the way she could support herself. Proud that she'd been so often tempted to take the easy way out and had steadfastly refused, even if it didn't look that way on paper if anyone dug deep enough.

She really didn't want Zeke Manning to ever want to look deep enough.

"That won't be necessary," she said, unable to keep the iciness out of her voice. She didn't follow up with a thank-you because she hardly felt any kind of appreciation for his offer.

Luckily, he didn't push it any further.

"What about you? Aren't you missing some important boardroom meetings?" she asked, to change the subject.

He laughed at her mocking tone. "I had my administrative assistant change my schedule so that I could do this."

"Why?"

"Why what?"

"Why is it so important to you?" She hadn't known she was going to press the matter, but something had been nagging at her about his determination to get Esther back the item that she owned. "I mean, I know it's technically your job." She bit her bottom lip, contemplating exactly how she wanted to ask the question. She decided it was best to just blurt out what was making her curious. "But you seem personally invested."

Zeke was silent for so long that the air between them grew thick and awkward. Eventually, rather than answer, he glanced at his watch. "I think we've ascended enough to have the food brought out." He pushed a button on his armrest and the flight attendant appeared within moments carrying a tray of steaming eggs, toast, various pastries and a silver carafe of aromatic coffee.

Vivi decided not to push, either. It appeared she wasn't the only one good at changing the subject of an uncomfortable conversation.

He'd been right about how intuitive Vivi was. Zeke couldn't recall anyone in his life who'd been able to read him at all. Yet here was this virtual stranger who seemed to be able to do just that. Maybe there was something to the idea that people could read cards, after all. Maybe someone like Vivi really had the kind of talent where she could look at illustrated pictures on a few cards and interpret what those pictures might mean for the person sitting across from her. Who was he to say?

"How long have you known Esther?" he asked her as she took a small bite of her toast. He wanted to get a better feel for this woman, wanted to know more about her. Asking about her relationship with their mutual friend seemed a good enough segue.

She swallowed the bite she'd taken before answering. "She came into the shop one day about six months ago. Just to browse and shop for souvenirs for her staff, she said. When she noticed my table, she asked for a reading. She started coming in once a week after that."

Zeke poured himself more coffee. They were both already on their second cup.

Vivi continued without further prompting. "One day she came in and said it would probably be her last time. That it was just too hard for her to make it into the French Quarter—she wasn't as mobile as she used to be, even with a driver. She seemed really sad about it."

He could extrapolate the rest. "So you offered to go to her."

Vivi set down her toast on the porcelain plate. "It wasn't a burden for me to take the trolley to her place. She didn't seem interested in the cards so much as she was the conversation. I got the impression she gets lonely."

"That was kind of you," Zeke told her, and he meant it. Not many twentysomethings would give up a part of their day once a week to spend it with an old woman looking for a companion.

A less-than-generous voice nagged in his mind that plenty of opportunists or fortune hunters would do just that. But he squelched that voice before it could grow louder. He'd decided yesterday that he'd give her the benefit of the doubt and he had no reason to go back on that decision. Not just yet, anyway.

She shrugged. "Like I said, it wasn't any kind of burden. Even if I wasn't getting paid for the 'reading,' quote unquote, that I was there for."

That took him by surprise. "What do you mean you weren't getting paid for the reading?"

"Esther said the staff, on the direction of her nephew, didn't allow her to write checks. She'd made too many mistakes. And she didn't want them handling her personal affairs, which she considered me a part of. I think she was embarrassed that she was paying someone to essentially just talk to her. Plus, it wasn't like I could swipe her card if we weren't at the shop. She also didn't keep much cash on the premises for obvious reasons."

"I see."

"That was why she liked to give me odd items from time to time. Because I wasn't officially getting paid."

Zeke rubbed his forehead. What an innocuous explanation. Both Esther's and Vivi's hearts had been in the right place. "It's why she mistakenly gave you a priceless necklace."

Vivi nodded, picked up an orange and started to peel. "That's right."

A wave of fresh guilt washed over Zeke as he listened to Vivi. Here was the explanation all along about how Vivi had come in possession of the necklace. All he'd had to do was ask. He should have done just that, asked Esther to explain to him exactly how this whole fiasco had come about. Instead, he'd stormed to Vivi's place of employment to confront her. No wonder she still held a grudge about it.

He had to make it up to her somehow. As soon as he could, he'd find a way.

CHAPTER SIX

VIVI COULDN'T QUITE describe the way Zeke was looking at her. But something about his gaze made her stomach tie in strange little knots. Suddenly, the air in the plane's main cabin felt warm and stuffy. She unbuttoned her cardigan and peeled it off. With all the nervous squirming in her chair earlier, the tank top she wore had ridden up above her belly button. Before she could pull its hem back down, Zeke's gaze fell to the blemish above her left hipbone that was the size of a quarter. Curiosity immediately filled the depths of his eyes.

Vivi sighed. The dermatologist had done the best she could. She'd had a rather amateur tattooist's work to deal with, however. "Go ahead and ask," she prompted Zeke, who was trying and failing in several attempts to not look at the spot.

"Only if you care to tell me," he said.

"I had a tattoo removed," she explained.

"Sometimes the procedure leaves a permanent scar."

He merely lifted one eyebrow in response.

"I'm guessing you don't have any tattoos," Vivi continued. "Let alone felt regretful enough to need to remove one."

He nodded once. "You would be guessing correctly."

"Yeah, well. It was the only one I've ever gotten." She tried not to grimace as the memory came flooding back. Todd urging her incessantly as he sat in the chair waiting for his scorpion to be colored in. Telling her how much it meant to him. Eventually, she'd succumbed to his less-than-gentle insistence. Hard to believe she'd ever been that impressionable, that downright stupid.

"Did you regret it right away?"

"Pretty much." Though it had taken her months to save up enough to pay for the doctor's visit. She was still paying off the remainder of what she owed.

She regretted the tattoo so much that she occasionally wore makeup to hide the blemish and wished she'd done so this morning. This wasn't a path of conversation she wanted to head down with the man sitting across from her.

"Let me guess," Zeke began. "A cute bumblebee. But one day not long after you got it, you were stung by one. And in your ire, you had it removed."

Vivi had to laugh at his guess. "One flaw in that theory. Bumblebees don't sting."

"Of course. A butterfly, then. But one day you tripped and fell as you were chasing one to admire it."

She chuckled again. "It wasn't an animal or insect," she clarified, not quite sure why she felt the need to. It was fun talking to Zeke. Despite their first meeting, he had a fun, easygoing style that somehow put her at ease. Even under these strange circumstances. "It wasn't a picture at all, in fact," she added.

He steepled his fingers in front of his chin. "I see. A word, then. A word you wanted removed from your person. So it had to be a name."

Vivi swallowed. He was too sharp by half. "Let's just say things didn't exactly work out with the bearer of said name."

That had to be the understatement of the year. The man had nearly destroyed her life. He'd certainly destroyed her reputation and left her with a criminal record.

For one insane moment, she wanted to tell Zeke all of it. She wanted to just confess and get it all off her chest in the hopes that he would be compassionate enough to understand. But she couldn't take that risk. He was being charming and pleasant right now, but she couldn't forget the angry man who had barged into the magic shop and confronted her with his accusations. Something told her the edginess he succeeded in holding at bay was all too close to the surface. A sleeping predator she didn't want to risk poking.

After all, Zeke was an attorney first and foremost. She had enough experience with them to know how things might play out if he found out the truth. No doubt, his first instinct would be to think the worst of her and notify the proper authorities about what he suspected. He'd probably consider it his professional duty.

In fact, she'd shared too much already. Zeke Manning didn't need to know one more thing about her past or her disastrous relationship.

Unclasping her seat belt, she stood up to momentarily step away from the conversation and from Zeke's all-too-observant eye. "I think I'd like to stretch my legs a bit—"

Before she got out the last word, the plane hit a turbulent bump hard enough to have her nearly toppling over. She windmilled her arms in a failed attempt to try and regain her balance. There was nothing for it, she was about to go down and probably take the breakfast tray with her.

But suddenly a set of strong, steadying arms had gripped her around the waist and she found herself colliding against Zeke's chest. How in the world had he moved so fast?

"I got you," he said softly, his breath warm against her cheek.

Vivi didn't need to look up to know how close his face was to hers. If she moved her head so much as half an inch, their lips would be a hair's width apart.

A mischievous, naughty voice inside her head told her to do just that. To succumb to the desire to see what a man like Zeke might taste like, how his mouth would feel on hers.

His frame felt strong and solid against her body, and she could feel his pulse pounding under his skin. Or maybe that was just her heart beating in her chest. It seemed to be throbbing double time.

"Uh, thanks," she muttered. "That could have been messy. I was heading right for the tray of food."

"And painful," he added.

His grip loosened ever so slightly and she felt a strange sense of loss and regret. Pushing past it, she slowly unfolded herself from his side and took a moment to compose herself. It wasn't easy.

"I think I'll do that stretching once we land," she said with a weak attempt at a smile as she sat back down. Her legs were wobbly, all right, but not because of any air pockets in the sky.

"Good idea," Zeke said, taking his own seat.

Vivi made a pronounced show of studying the view of the clouds outside the small oval window. What had just happened between them? Whatever it was, it couldn't happen again.

She just had to keep her head together and her wits about her until they got back to New Orleans. She's made too many mistakes in the past when it came to falling for the wrong man. She couldn't do that again. It had taken her too long to put her life back together to risk it all now.

But there was no denying the fact that she'd wanted to kiss him back there. And, heaven help her, she still did.

Vivi's resolve to maintain a physical distance from Zeke grew only harder when they landed and entered the private town car that would take them to Niagara Falls. Her heart had only just now reached a normal, resting state. By contrast, Zeke seemed completely unaffected by what had transpired between them. Or almost transpired. Not that she should be surprised. This was the man who had offered to compensate her for her time this morning. He viewed her as nothing more than some kind of employee. While she was still out of sorts about the way it had felt to be in his arms, he'd probably forgotten about the incident completely.

She studied him now as they drove away from the airport and the driver merged onto the expressway. Zeke had his tablet open and was typing furiously on the keyboard.

"I apologize," he said without looking up from the screen. "I don't mean to be rude, but I have to fire off some emails before we get to our destination. I'm due in France in a few days to oversee an estate sale, a family winery that's being bought out by a US conglomerate. Some of the paperwork is having lost-in-translation issues."

"You don't have to entertain me," Vivi told him. What a life he must lead. In just a week's span he would be traveling from New Orleans to Europe with a cursory stop in between where she was accompanying him. And here she was almost giddy to be able to fly to one of the great natural wonders of the world.

"Almost done. Sorry," Zeke said in a conciliatory tone.

"There's no need to apologize for trying to get your work done."

"Hmm," he replied absentmindedly, still not looking up.

Yep, he was barely aware of her presence. Whereas sitting in such close quarters with him was wreaking havoc on her senses. They were in much closer proximity now than they had been on the plane and that had been close enough.

"I'll try Roxie one more time." Vivi pulled out her phone just to give herself something to do. Though she knew the task was futile. Roxie had yet to answer several texts and voice mails Vivi had left since last night. For all she knew, the other woman had locked up her phone in the hotel room's safe to focus solely on her honeymoon.

To be that enamored with a man. Would she ever know how that might feel?

Like a fool, when she'd first met Todd, Vivi had entertained the possibility that she might finally have someone in her corner, someone she might pursue a future with. Instead, he'd very nearly destroyed her future altogether.

Now her gaze shifted to the man sitting across from her. She got the feeling countless women had been enamored with Zeke Manning over the years. A bunch of them probably still were.

She sucked in a breath. It could be argued that Vivi was headed in that same direction and might even be counted among that group.

She shook off the thought. She was just being silly. It was no wonder she felt drawn to someone like him. Compared to her last boyfriend, or anyone else she'd dated, for that matter, he was a whole separate breed.

Smart, successful, well educated. He had material wealth that he'd obviously worked hard for and led the kind of life most men would admire. *Focus*.

She made herself look away from Zeke's profile and concentrated on hitting the redial button on Roxie's contact entry. The same three chords sounded immediately through the speaker, followed by the same annoying automated message.

And now the voice-mail box was full.

Great. They would have to follow their original plan. Head to the chapel Roxie's mom had provided and check the handful of hotels nearby where the newlyweds might be staying.

"No luck, huh?"

Vivi looked up to find Zeke had put away his tablet and was focused solely on her now. Only a foot apart on the seat, his closeness was really starting to feel disconcerting. She liked it better when he was distracted with work.

"I'm afraid not," she answered, then focused her attention out the window. Outside the glass there was just so much green. All that grass and lush trees for miles. She'd grown up near the French Quarter. Sure, there were parks and fields in New Orleans, but she'd never seen such a long stretch of shrubbery as far as the eye could see.

She wasn't in Louisiana anymore.

"Penny for them," Zeke prompted. "Your thoughts, that is."

"I was just admiring the view," she answered vaguely. "The scenery out here is lovely." The comment was a bit of a fib. It was much too quiet out this way. Where was everybody? The small houses that dotted the side of the road had no one outside in the yards. Porches were well-kept but empty.

She thought about how busy the streets would be back home this time in the afternoon. All the crowds mixed up of tourists and locals alike. Music would play from every angle.

"If you think it's pretty out here, wait until you see the falls," Zeke said.

"What's it like? Majestic, I bet." Probably breathtaking, she added mentally. "I've gone hiking in Carrs Creek, which has a few, but I'm guessing those would look like a trickle in comparison."

"I've only been here a handful of times myself. But you're right. It's hard to describe. There's just so much water."

The way he said the last word had her giggling once again. "Yes, that's typically what waterfalls are composed of. Hence the name."

He chuckled along with her. "You'll see what I mean when we get there."

She hesitated to voice her next thought. Then decided she'd just bite the bullet. When would she ever get a chance again to come back out this way?

Probably never, was the most likely answer. Clearing her throat, she began her question. "I know we're not exactly here on a pleasure trip. But maybe we could spend some time sightseeing? The pictures I saw of the falls online were breathtaking. I'd love to see it up close if possible."

Zeke's grin spread wide and she had to suck in a breath at the responding reaction in her middle. "Say no more," he answered, giving her a playful wink.

Zeke didn't want to examine too closely why he'd agreed so quickly to Vivi's suggestion just now. After all, what was he supposed to do? Look into those rich, deep hazel eyes and turn her down? The woman simply wanted to spend some time admiring one of the most memorable wonders on earth. He'd be a monster to say no.

Right. Like that was the only reason he'd agreed.

Recalling the way she'd felt in his arms had his skin tingling. This was bad. Things had gone much too far. He was attracted to her. Like he'd never been toward another woman. He had to admit that.

The smart thing to do would have been to ask the driver to take her where she wanted to go while he got some work done in the hotel room until they located the wayward couple who had Esther's necklace. Heaven knew he had enough to do. He was due in France in a few days to finalize the estate transfer for a winery. As much as he loved visiting the French countryside, this was one trip he wasn't looking forward to. First, this little wild-goose chase to upstate New York had thrown quite a wrench in his schedule. Second, the winery owners insisted on trying to set him up with their middle-aged single daughter. Zeke was running out of ways to politely decline their innuendos and the woman's unwelcome advances.

Well, there was no point in dwelling on any of it now. He'd already made his promise to Vivi. As for the pushy French winery owners, he would deal with that when the time came.

He packed up his tablet and shrugged on his jacket as the car pulled into the circular driveway of the hotel they'd be staying at. Zeke was hoping they wouldn't be here more than a day, but he'd booked a couple of rooms just in case. Worst-case scenario was he and Vivi might have to leave empty-handed. He honestly didn't know where they might go from there. The authorities would probably have to get involved at that point.

If that happened, Zeke would wash his hands of the whole matter. Of course, he'd check in on Esther from time to time. But there was only so much he could do. He'd leave New Orleans not knowing when he might return.

His gaze shifted to the woman accompanying him. One way or another, this little adventure they were currently on would be over. The thought brought a pang of regret along with it. He'd never met anyone like Vivienne Ducarne. Probably never would again. There was no doubt she'd been burned in the past. The erased tattoo was proof of that. And she clearly hadn't led the easiest life. But she didn't seem bitter or hardened in any way. No, she was definitely soft. All over. He knew firsthand.

Zeke squeezed his eyes shut. He couldn't go there again. Had to make sure to keep his hands off her.

Geography aside, Vivi wasn't the type of woman he could pursue any kind of relationship with. She was too free-spirited, too unpredictable. She had no clear goals that he could see, despite having immense potential as a gifted jazz singer. Zeke needed more structure in his existence—the woman he needed in his life would be as committed to a life of stability as he was or it would never work. And, as tempting as it was, Zeke had never been one for flings or one-night stands. It just wasn't in his nature. No, he and Vivi were only here for one thing—to retrieve the necklace and return it to its rightful owner.

Everything else was just a distraction he didn't need.

Hopefully, she didn't take any more stumbles and literally fall into his arms again. Not that he'd complained. She'd smelled of fruity shampoo and fresh clean soap. In fact, the scent of her had tickled in his nostrils in the tight confines of the car. An alluring and flowery scent that was distinctively her own.

Enough, already.

As soon as the car came to a stop, Zeke wasted no time in opening his door and hopping out. The driver was already at the other side, assisting Vivi out of the vehicle.

"I thought we could freshen up a bit before we head out and start asking about Roxie and her groom."

"All right."

She paused suddenly before they reached the revolving doors that led to the hotel lobby.

"That sound? Is that…?"

He had to smile at the look of wonder on her face. "Yes. It's the falls. It can be heard from more than a mile away."

"That's incredible. I can't wait to see it."

Zeke realized with a start just how much he wanted that, too. More accurately, he wanted to see *her* as she saw the falls, silly as it sounded. Looking around them, it was hard not to notice the many couples strolling in and out of the hotel. Many held hands or walked snuggled tight up against each other.

This city really did attract newlyweds like bees to a hive. It was hard not to feel somewhat envious. Though he knew that made no sense at all. He wasn't looking for any kind of relationship, knew he wasn't equipped for any kind of long-term union, let alone marriage. Not with the kind of baggage he carried. These useless wayward thoughts really needed to stop.

"I already said we would, didn't I?" he answered rather curtly, madder at himself than Vivi's excitement. She seemed taken aback but didn't respond. Just as well.

"Come on. We should go check in."

Silently, she followed him into the lobby, where they were greeted at the main desk by a dapper-looking attendant with a pencil-thin mustache and a friendly smile below it.

Zeke gave him the reservation number.

"One key or two, sir?" the other man asked.

The question made no sense. "I don't understand," Zeke admitted. "We were supposed to have two separate rooms."

Had his administrative assistant misunderstood the request? The woman was a relatively new hire—he should have followed up.

"Apologies, sir," the attendant began. "They are indeed two separate rooms. But they are adjoined by a common suite with one entry door."

Without asking again, he handed Zeke and Vivi each a separate plastic key card.

Vivi stiffened ever so slightly next to him but took the card without comment. Zeke wasn't going to bother arguing the situation with the staff. It wasn't worth it. All that mattered was that they had two separate rooms. It wasn't as if they would be sharing one. They didn't even need to see each other when they were indoors.

And if the temptation to step into the common area in the hope that she might also be there became too much, he would just have to ignore it.

How hard could it be?

CHAPTER SEVEN

VIVI NEARLY FELL running out of the shower when she heard the ding of her cell phone. The alert sound was the one she'd assigned to text messages. Roxie! Finally!

But when she finally reached it, she saw it was just a short message from Bessa asking how their flight had gone. Wait until she told her friend how different a private jet was than flying commercial. Before she had a chance to respond, her phone rang with an incoming call. Zeke, this time.

"Hello, Zeke."

"Hey, there. What do you think about heading out? Have you had enough time to freshen up?"

Vivi looked about the luxurious room she'd walked into about forty-five minutes ago. She'd spent about a third of that time just lying on the large, sumptuous bed, staring at the patterned ceiling.

Zeke hadn't given her any kind of time window and now she was standing here dripping wet with her hair a mess of tangles.

She'd lingered in the shower, too. But it was so hard to leave the large marble stall with the scented bodywash and waterproof radio that had been streaming music from her favorite app. Oh, and also the showerhead with six different settings that ranged from "massage" to "gentle mist."

A girl could get used to this.

"Vivi? You still there?"

She shook her head. "Um. I could use a few more minutes. I was in the shower."

"Take your time. I'll be waiting for you," he said before disconnecting.

A shiver ran along her spine as she tossed her phone on the bed. It had nothing to do with being soaking wet in an air-conditioned hotel room. No, it was more the tone of Zeke's voice and the exact words he'd used.

I'll be waiting for you.

Vivi knew she was being silly. There was absolutely no reason to read in anything to Zeke simply telling her that he'd be patient while she got ready. But her mind couldn't help but replay an imaginary scenario where she was one of the women they'd passed by on their way through the hotel. A new bride. One whose groom was waiting for her as she got dressed. Against her will, her mind replayed the previous night in the club, when he'd held her in his arms as they swayed to the music.

She blew out a breath and plopped down on the bed, then rolled over onto her stomach. The duvet smelled freshly laundered, with the scent of lavender. The sooner she got those pictures out of her head, the better. Logic dictated that she wasn't about to be a bride anytime soon. And certainly not one wed to the likes of someone like Ezekiel Manning.

Zeke shoved his phone back into his pocket and tried to push away the images that were running through his head. Images of Vivi in a steamy hot shower, soap suds slowly moving over her curves. Water cascading over her skin.

Stop. It. Now.

What was wrong with him? He was acting like a hormonal high-school student with his first crush. He needed some air.

He threw open his door and strode through the common sitting area of their suite, making his way to the balcony. A sunny bright sky greeted him when he stepped outside. A fine sheen of mist hung in the air from the waterfall in the distance. He breathed in deep, trying to make sense of the myriad of emotions pummeling his center.

He didn't have time for the complication of being so attracted to Vivienne Ducarne. His life was finally one of order and normality. He was his own boss, made a very decent living and had a contact list full of willing women he could call when he wanted companionship.

Vivi would never be one of those women. First of all, he doubted she would be up for any kind of fling. He might not have known her for long, but he'd grown to know her enough to surmise that much. Not that he'd ever consider asking her.

No, once they left Niagara Falls, he would have to be on his way back home and leave Vivi completely and unequivocally behind him.

Just like so much of his past. And also like his past, it was for the best. He repeated those last five words like a mantra as he watched the pedestrian traffic in the square below. Yet more couples. A few families mixed in for good measure. Did no one single ever come to this town by themselves?

Several moments passed before he heard light footsteps behind him.

"Something down there making you out of sorts?" she asked from over his shoulder, peering down past the railing.

He hadn't realized he'd sworn out loud. "Just mentally kicking myself for a mistake I made earlier," he answered. That was the complete truth.

"You should go easier on yourself. People make mistakes," she said, her voice tight.

Was it his imagination or was there more to her words than small talk?

"Yes. They do. Some mistakes are bigger than others, however."

"Can't argue with you there." He was about to stand up so they could get going, but she pulled out the other lounge chair and dropped down into it. She'd changed into a light navy blue wraparound dress with tiny red roses dotting the fabric. The color brought out the tanned bronze of her skin and the dark strands of her hair.

On her feet, she still wore the same comfortable-looking sneakers that shouldn't have worked with such a dressy outfit, but somehow on her they worked. Not that he was any kind of fashion expert.

She continued, "For instance, when a sweet, little old lady gifts you a glittery necklace and you don't so much as question it. That was clearly a mistake."

She wasn't wrong. But Zeke's first thought was that he'd have never met her otherwise. Regardless of how this situation played out, whether he ever saw her again after, he was glad to know her. Not something he was about to admit out loud.

"Hopefully we'll be able to rectify that while we're here," he said instead.

She tilted her head toward him, staring out at the horizon. "Silver lining. I get to see a part of the country I never planned on visiting."

"I'm glad for that, Vivi." He turned to fully face her. There was something that had been tugging at him since last night on the steamship. "If you don't mind my asking, why haven't you left Louisiana?"

She shrugged. "It's my home. What else would I do?"

"I've heard you sing, Vivi. I'm no expert but I think you've got a rare skill that should be pursued."

"I do pursue it. I sing on a busy steamboat tour on the lovely Mississippi."

"Don't you think your talent warrants more than that?"

"People from all over the world hear me perform."

"You could have so much more than that. Aren't you even curious about how far you could go?"

Vivi didn't answer, just started picking at a loose thread along the hem of her dress. He knew he might be overstepping but felt compelled to try and explain where he was coming from. "I just don't understand why anyone would bounce from one job to another, simply to try and make ends meet, when they have the means to pursue a real career. And you certainly do, Vivi. You sing like an angel."

She released a deep sigh. "I appreciate the compliment, Zeke. I really do."

Funny, she didn't sound as if she appreciated what he'd said in the least bit.

"I was a toddler when the elderly aunt who'd been looking after me passed," she continued. "I bounced around in foster care after that until I turned eighteen. The life I have now is more than I could have hoped for. I know that's something somebody like you wouldn't understand."

"You might be surprised."

She quirked an eyebrow. "Yeah? How so?"

"Let's just say I couldn't really have imagined the life I have now, either."

"Huh" was all she said in response.

"Don't you ever wonder if your vocal talent might lead you to even more?"

She studied him before responding, then effectively changed the subject. "We should probably get going."

There was more to her story. He just knew it. He also knew she wasn't going to share any more. Her desire to end the conversation had come through loud and clear.

He would drop the subject, as she wanted, and was rather sorry he'd ever brought it up.

Vivi was afraid to study Zeke's expression too closely as they walked out of the lobby and through the square. She wouldn't be able to stand it if he pitied her. The excitement she'd felt about seeing the falls had waned after their conversation on the balcony. She knew she shouldn't let it get to her, but she couldn't seem to help herself.

He cleared his throat as they meandered through the other tourists. "I'm sorry if I over-stepped. I was just very impressed with your voice and your ability when I heard you sing last night."

"Thank you," she said simply.

"I won't bring it up again."

But it was too late, wasn't it? The discussion hung in the air between them now. He thought she was unambitious, with no goals. Well, goals and ambition weren't meant for women like her. She was just aiming for survival.

A career in the spotlight was the last thing she needed or wanted. A life of fame or fortune wasn't in the cards for Vivienne Ducarne. Not with the skeletons she had in her closet. The less attention she called to herself, the better.

There was no way to explain that to Zeke without revealing those skeletons to him.

"So, truce?" he asked.

"I didn't realize we were at battle."

"More of a standoff, then."

Vivi did her best to shake off her irritation. "Whatever you want to call it, consider it over." For now, anyway.

The crowd around them grew larger and larger as they made their way down the sidewalk and crossed the street. Most everyone was headed in the same direction. The humming sound of the falls increased, so they had to be getting close.

"We must be almost there."

Zeke chuckled at her enthusiasm. "Slow down, I can barely keep up with you."

She hadn't even realized she'd quickened her stride. Finally they turned a corner and there it was. The pictures she'd seen online had not done the view justice. There was no comparing this to anything she'd seen on her hikes back in Louisiana.

It was unlike anything she could have imagined.

A massive sheet of water plunging over the edge like it was alive. A colorful rainbow glimmered at the base, rising high up into the air. A sheen of mist dampened her skin and clothes.

She moved closer to the railing, breathing deeply of the moist, refreshing air. *Majestic* was the only word that came to mind.

"What do you think?" Zeke asked softly in her ear as he reached her side.

She couldn't find the words to answer his question. There was no way to adequately describe what she was looking at. Like a child, she climbed the bottom rail and gripped the top one, leaned over as far as she could, nearly toppling over in the process.

"Whoa. Careful there," Zeke cautioned, grabbing her about the waist to steady her.

The scene quite literally took her breath away.

He was zero for two.

First he'd upset her by asking about her singing. Then he'd broken his vow to avoid touching her. That second one he could be forgiven for. He had been trying to save her from falling over a metal fence, after all. Never mind that his hands had lingered on her waist a second or two longer than needed.

Now they were making their way along the paved pathway trailing the viewing area of the American Falls. They'd been there close to an hour and Vivi didn't seem to be tiring of the excursion in any way.

"This is just awe-inspiring," she proclaimed, stopping to face the falls and admire it yet again.

He would have thought she'd run out of adjectives by now.

As awe-inspiring as the scenery was, Zeke was ready to call an end to the outing. Duty called and all. Plus, he was starting to get hungry. His time in New Orleans, with all its wonderful cuisine, had trained his stomach to expect rather frequent meals.

"How about we grab a bite?" he asked.

Vivi's face fell. "Already?"

As if on cue, his stomach grumbled loud enough to be heard over the rushing water. She chuckled in response. "I guess that's my answer."

"We're here for a while yet. We can always come back."

Her expression looked doubtful. How many people had broken their promises to Vivi over the span of her lifetime? "I'm a man of my word. We'll come back if you'd like."

"Okay. But one more picture." She pulled out her phone and aimed the screen.

Zeke stepped over to her, held his hand out for her phone. "Here. Let me. You should be in it."

She placed it in his hand just as an older couple approached them with wide, friendly smiles. "Let us take the photo," the woman offered. "We'll get both of you. You should have a couple's photo in front of that beautiful view."

Vivi immediately began to correct her. "Oh, there's no need. We're not actual—" But the lady wasn't listening.

"Nonsense." She took the phone out of Zeke's hand. "I'm Marge. Go stand together in front of the water."

Marge sure was a bossy sort.

Zeke gave Vivi a pointed look, one that hopefully conveyed the message that it was probably easier just to comply and move on with their day. Vivi must have gotten the hint. She nodded with a smile and followed Zeke to the railing.

Zeke did his best to pose as an adoring boyfriend/husband without actually making physical contact. It wasn't easy. Luckily, neither Marge nor her husband seemed to notice.

Several snaps later, they thanked the older couple and started making their way back to town.

"What are you in the mood for?" Zeke asked her, trying to recall which eating establishments they'd passed along the way.

"What's this area known for?"

"Burgers and hot dogs—believe it or not. And root-beer floats."

"You know what they say, when in Rome…"

Within minutes they were ordering at the window of a sidewalk diner with outdoor seating. Zeke ordered burgers and franks for both of them and a large basket of fries to share. They each carried a large plastic red tray laden with food and plenty of napkins.

"This should get me to my quota of grease for the month," Vivi remarked as they sat and began to eat. She moaned with pleasure after the first bite. Did the same after eating her first fry.

How did the woman make eating fast food look so darn sexy? Zeke made himself look away and focused instead on his hot dog.

"We should head to the chapel after this," Vivi said between bites.

He nodded in response. "It's as good a place as any to start. See if we can chart Roxie and Rocky's path."

"And if we can't find them?" she asked, dabbing a fry in a mound of runny ketchup. Worry laced her voice.

"Let's hope we get lucky."

She harrumphed out a humorless laugh. Zeke got the impression she wasn't used to seeing much luck come her way. Maybe one day he'd get her full story. But he wasn't about to ask now, not after the fiasco with asking about her potential singing career.

Zeke polished off his frank and moved on to the burger. But Vivi seemed to have lost her appetite.

"Do you want something else? I know this isn't exactly refined fare."

Another ironic laugh. "Refined is overrated. It's not that."

"Then what? Aren't you hungry?"

"I would just feel bad if we can't get Esther back what's rightfully hers."

He patted her hand. "Don't worry. One way or another that necklace will find its way where it belongs."

She mumbled something under her breath he couldn't quite make out. Zeke stood. This wouldn't do. She'd barely eaten anything, and they had a long afternoon ahead of them still. "I'll be right back," he told her and went back to the ordering window.

He returned with a large root-beer float in a tall plastic stein and two long straws. "Dessert," he announced.

"I'm rather full…" Vivi protested, but her words held no real conviction.

"Come on," he prodded. "Who can resist the combination of creamy ice cream and bubbly, sugary soda?"

She clasped a hand to her chest with a dramatic shake of her head. "Not I."

He set the concoction in front of her and pulled a chair close. Even with the scent of grease and sugar lingering in the air, he could still smell the fruity fragrance of her hair. He had to clench his fists tightly to resist leaning in and inhaling deeply the alluring scent that had now become so familiar. Being close to her always seemed to wreak havoc on his senses.

For the life of him, he didn't know what to do about it.

CHAPTER EIGHT

An hour after their salt-and-sugar-laden lunch, they headed back toward the square. The chapel was in the center of town. Vivi hoped for the best. But now that she thought about it, what were the odds they would actually locate Roxie and her new husband? Niagara Falls was bigger than she would have thought. And it was crawling with tourists, domestic and from other countries. Just on their walk right now, she could hear a myriad of different languages and accents.

Finding anyone in such a setting seemed to be the proverbial needle-in-a-haystack scenario.

Somehow, Zeke seemed to have read her thoughts. "Have faith, Vivi. Don't assume failure yet."

"How do you know that's what I was doing?"

He motioned to her, waving his hand up and down. "You've got your hands clasped in front of your middle and you've gone stiff as a board. It's not hard to tell you're stressed."

"I'm starting to wonder how feasible it is to think we might find them among this crowd of people."

"One task at a time. Assume success until proven otherwise."

Quite the lesson in how to approach life. "Is that how you've achieved all your success? With that motto?"

He shrugged. "That and sheer determination. I had a lot to prove."

To whom? Vivi wondered. Maybe the world in general.

Within minutes, they'd reached the small brick building that housed the Niagara Bridal Chapel. A colorful sign hung by the door that read: No appointment necessary. First come, first served.

"Not much different than how we ordered lunch earlier."

"Not everyone's into ceremony," Zeke said.

"Or they just can't wait to get married."

A matronly middle-aged woman with her gray hair piled high in a bun atop her head greeted them as soon as they opened the door.

"Come in! Come in! So nice to have you."

Zeke guided Vivi forward and introduced them both.

"I'm Penny," the woman replied. "Apologies,

we're running a little behind, but the minister will be here in just a moment."

She glanced down at Vivi's empty hands with something of a frown. "Let me get you a bouquet." She pivoted on her heel before Vivi could process exactly what was happening.

"I'm afraid we only have plastic flowers," Penny added over her shoulder.

Horror washed over her as realization dawned. Before she could stop the other woman, a gentleman in a dark suit and neck collar appeared through the door.

"Welcome. Let's get started, shall we?"

"No!" Vivi and Zeke both yelled in unison. The minister startled and Penny stopped in her tracks, a bouquet of fake flowers in her hands.

"That's not why we're here," Zeke quickly explained.

"Hmm," Penny said. "Why else would you be in a chapel at two o'clock in the afternoon? In Niagara Falls?"

Zeke stepped forward. "Sorry for the confusion. We're actually looking for some friends of ours. We were told this is where they eloped."

Penny's lips thinned with disapproval. "We don't use that term here, sir. Every marriage is sacred, and we pride ourselves on providing a quality ceremony for all our couples."

"Of course. I apologize," Zeke offered with a slight conciliatory bow.

"We happen to be in town and we wanted to congratulate them," Vivi added. It was true enough.

Between the two of them, they managed to give a quick summary that left out anything about a priceless necklace, so that it didn't sound as crazy as the truth actually was.

The minister rubbed his jaw when they were done. "I don't know. We get a lot of couples through here."

"My friend has fiery red hair," Vivi said. "And her new husband wears his hair in a po-nytail. Sometimes a man bun."

"That could describe a third of the couples we've had in here in the last week," Penny said with a click of her tongue.

"They would have been in here yesterday. Maybe the day before."

The minister squinted his eyes in concentra-tion.

"Maybe the names will help," Zeke said. "Roxie and Rocky."

That seemed to do the trick. Both the minister and Penny nodded in recognition. "Of course!" the man said. "I remember them. Thought they were joking about the names until I saw their paperwork."

"They were a hoot!" Penny added. "Lovely couple."

"Those two couldn't keep their hands off each other," the minister told them. "Even more so than the usual couples we get in here," he added with a wink.

That certainly explained why Roxie couldn't be bothered to pick up her phone or check her messages.

"Do you happen to remember where they said they were staying?" Zeke asked. "So we can send them a bottle of champagne with our congratulations."

"I think they said the Borderside Inn," Penny answered.

The minister shook his head in disagreement. "No, I don't think so. I think they said Niagara Nightly."

"That's okay." Zeke told him. "We'll try both." He extended his hand to shake the minister's. "You've both been very helpful."

Vivi nodded her thanks as well, then followed Zeke out the door with a nearly overwhelming sense of relief. Maybe they'd be able to find the necklace after all. It was just like Zeke had advised earlier: assume success until proven otherwise.

A bubble of laughter escaped her lips as they stepped back out into the sunshine.

"What's so funny?" Zeke asked.

Vivi sat down on the front steps—she just needed a second to gather her thoughts. The whole day had been one continuous whirlwind. "First of all, I can't believe that actually worked. Second, we were almost married just now."

Zeke sat down next to her on the concrete step, bumped her shoulder with his own playfully. "Maybe I should call you almost-wife from now on."

A wayward thought popped into her head at his joking suggestion. Her stomach quivered with an achy longing at the term. *Almost-wife.* Saints above, but it had a nice ring to it.

They decided to try the Borderside Inn first. It was closest of the two places Penny and the minister had mentioned and conveniently on the way back to their own hotel. A buffet was set up out in the lobby when they arrived about ten minutes later. The place was quaint and charming. Zeke figured it did well enough, given its location. It certainly seemed to be full now. Several children scurried about, so the place clearly attracted families as well as honeymooners. Not that that was any kind of useful fact he might need. Zeke didn't really have any family and he certainly had no plans to become a honeymooner anytime soon.

His gaze drifted to the woman next to him and scenes he had no business imagining flooded his mind before he pushed them away. A solitary attendant worked the front desk, so it took them a while to get past the line of guests checking in and out. Finally it was their turn.

Zeke summoned his most charming smile as the woman greeted him. The silver nameplate she wore said *Mindy* in curvy black lettering.

"Good afternoon. I was hoping you might help us with a gift. I wanted to send a bottle of your finest champagne to two of your guests. They just got married. But I don't happen to know their room number."

Mindy returned his smile with a warm one of her own. "Oh, how lovely of you. That's not a problem." She clicked away at her keyboard. "Just give me the last name."

Vivi stepped in. "Clairmont. Roxie Clairmont."

Mindy clicked away some more, but then her warm smile turned downward. Zeke felt a tightening in his gut. The woman's expression did not look promising. "Hmm," she began. "I'm not seeing anyone checked in here under that name."

"What's Rocky's last name?" he asked Vivi. "Maybe they used his."

If they were even at the right hotel. Vivi

gave him a blank look. Zeke resisted the urge to swear out loud. To have come this far only to be sidelined because they didn't have even the most basic of facts…

"I'm really sorry," Mindy said with a woeful look at each of them in turn. "I can't find the room without a last name. Wish I could help."

Zeke released the curse he'd been holding in as soon as they stepped away from the desk.

"I have an idea," Vivi said when they reached the lounge area by the glass double doors of the entrance. "I'll text Bessa so that she can text Roxie's mom and ask what Rocky's last name is."

He must have gone to sleep the other night and woken up in a sitcom. So many degrees of separation.

"There's just one problem," Vivi added.

Of course there was. "Bessa's at work at the Crawdad. Where she doesn't have—"

"Access to her phone," Zeke said, completing the sentence for her.

Honestly, were people from Louisiana just not as attached to their phones as the rest of the country? Roxie wasn't even answering hers.

"Go ahead and give it a try," he told her. Not like they had any other options.

She sent the text then slipped the phone back

into her cross-body purse. "Guess now we just wait and see."

"May as well take a walk outside," Zeke suggested. "This hotel happens to be behind one of those rose gardens this part of the country is known for."

Vivi gave a noncommittal shrug. "Sure. Why not. May as well look at some beauty while we wait."

Zeke didn't say out loud what he was thinking. That he'd been looking at something beautiful since this morning. Their quick jaunt from the chapel to the hotel had brought a hint of red to her cheeks, bringing out the golden hazel of her eyes. The humidity of this climate had added gentle curls to her dark hair. Her skin seemed to glow with the sheen of mist from the falls in the air. And the way she smelled. He couldn't seem to get enough of that fruity scent. It reminded him of lazy afternoons in the tropics.

What in the world was wrong with him? He was usually not the type to daydream about a woman's looks or the tone of her skin. It must be the effect of being around all these newlyweds and besotted-looking couples.

They followed the signs down a wooden pathway by the side of the inn that directed them to the rose garden. When they reached the entry gate, Zeke realized what an inadequate name that was for the place. There were certainly roses, but a variety of bushes bearing other flowers dotted the landscape.

"Wow." The simple comment came from Vivi. She looked almost as impressed as she'd been at the Horseshoe Falls earlier.

The colors alone were enough to take away anyone's breath. But what was really noteworthy was the pleasing scent of several floral varieties that filled the air.

"It's like we've stepped into some kind of Eden," Vivi commented.

A bucket of roses for sale sat by a nearby bench. Zeke threw several bills in the payment bin and handed one to Vivi. "A piece of Eden for you, then."

Vivi took the long-stemmed red rose and inhaled deeply. Something squeezed in his middle. The look of pure pleasure on her face had his senses tingling. He could put that look on her face. He could bring her pleasure and take what she had to give in return. A slight breeze rippled the air and blew several strands of curls onto her cheek. Zeke couldn't seem to help himself. He reached over and gently tucked a strand back behind her ear.

What was that vow about not touching her again?

He really needed to pull his hand away from where it still lingered at the base of her delicate ear. But she looked up at him, and heaven help him, he saw the same desire shining in her eyes. She tilted her head up toward him, bringing their lips a needle's breadth apart. Thoughts of any kind of self-imposed vow flew out of his head. Before he could allow himself to think, he lowered his mouth onto hers and finally indulged in what he'd been fantasizing about for so long.

She tasted as good as he'd been imagining. And, oh, had he imagined it. Probably since that first time he'd laid eyes on her. She tasted of berries and honey, like a delectable exotic candied berry. A slow moan escaped her mouth under his lips and he thought it might be his undoing. The kiss was suddenly deeper, more wanton. He couldn't even tell which one of them had caused it.

They were interrupted when a shadow fell over them where they sat on the bench. Someone cleared their throat softly above their heads. With nearly painful reluctance, Zeke made himself pull away from her. Mindy, from the main desk. "I've been looking everywhere for you two. I asked my colleague about your friends. He knew exactly who you were referring to."

It took several moments to regain any sense

of thought, or to even process what the woman was saying. Then he remembered why he and Vivi were even there in the first place.

Vivi managed to find her voice first. "He did?"

Mindy nodded with enthusiasm. "He knew right away when I mentioned their first names. He checked them in and recalls which room they're in. Would you like to send them that champagne now?"

Vivi was finding it hard to focus as they followed the hotel's front-desk attendant back to the main lobby. She knew this was cause for relief. They'd managed to find the proverbial needle in the haystack! But all she could think about right now was the way it had felt to be in Zeke's arms. How he had tasted against her lips. The pleasure he'd made her feel deep in her core. She couldn't recall ever reacting to a man's kiss with such abandon. She still felt the tingle along all her nerve endings. Her heart still pounded in her chest.

She squeezed her eyes shut. Right now they had a more pressing matter. They were about to finally get that cursed necklace back.

Vivi waited as the arrangements for the champagne were made and Zeke handed Mindy his credit card. "Could you send my friend a message along with the gift?"

"Of course!" Mindy immediately agreed.

"Could you please tell her to check her voice mail and that we're down here to see them? We'll be in the lobby when they're ready."

The other woman blinked in confusion but then simply gave a small shrug. "I'll make sure they get your message," she assured them.

"Looks like we're in yet another holding pattern," Zeke remarked after they'd moved back to the lounge area of the lobby. Had he been as affected by their kiss as she was? That certainly didn't seem to be the case. He looked calm and collected. As if nothing had happened.

While her stomach was still overrun with butterflies.

She was still clutching the rose he'd given her in her fingers. How did a man give a woman a rose, kiss her silly the next instant and then only moments later act as if nothing had happened?

The better question was, why was she exerting any of her energy right now on anything but getting Esther's necklace back?

She paced from one corner of the lobby to the other, her thoughts a jumbled mess darting between that mind-blowing kiss and the astounding fact that they'd finally found Roxie and her groom.

Vivi didn't know how much time had passed before she heard the ding of the elevator arriving followed by a very familiar Southern twang.

"Oh, my God, Vivi. Are you playing some kind of prank on me?"

Roxie, clad in a long silk robe with a feather collar, jogged across the lobby to where she and Zeke waited. She gave Vivi a shoulder squeeze in greeting then gave Zeke a swift nod of acknowledgement.

"No prank, Roxie. I'm so sorry for the misunderstanding. But we need that necklace back."

"Of course. Heavens. This is so hard to believe. My heart jumped to my throat when I finally listened to your messages." She slammed a hand to her chest. "When I think about how careless I've been with it."

She motioned for them to follow her. "Come on up. Rocky's getting dressed."

Yep, they'd certainly interrupted a couple on their honeymoon.

"This is Zeke," Vivi said when they were all in the elevator.

"Hey there, sugar. Thanks for the champagne."

"It's the least we could do. So sorry for interrupting your honeymoon."

Roxie waved off his apology.

"He's the estate attorney who discovered what Esther had done," Vivi explained.

Roxie shook her head slowly from side to side. "That poor woman. She just wasn't thinking straight, huh?"

"No. She wasn't."

"Well, all that matters is we get her rightful property back to her."

The inflection of Zeke's tone held just enough of a hint of accusation that it gave Vivi pause. Surely, he wasn't blaming Roxie for any of this. The poor woman had had no idea. She'd simply accepted a wedding gift from a friend.

In case Zeke hadn't noticed, Vivi and her circle of friends weren't exactly the type of crew who would recognize a priceless antique when they saw one.

"You can have it back," Roxie told them. "It's giving me hives to think I had something that valuable in my possession all this time."

When they got to the hotel room, Rocky was waiting for them with the door open. The men quickly shook hands.

"So this isn't some kind of prank, then?" Rocky asked, his accent thick Louisiana Creole.

"I'm afraid not."

Roxie went to the bureau and pulled out a drawer. Finally, she lifted out the object that had caused so much angst and rushed it over to Zeke. She handed it to him with a visible shudder.

"Thank you."

"No problem."

The exchange was so normal that Vivi couldn't help but think how anticlimactic all of it was. But like Zeke said, all that mattered was getting the darned thing back where it belonged.

"Here." Rocky handed them a velvet bag with a thick drawstring. "Don't forget its container."

Vivi took Roxie in her arms and enveloped her in a tight hug. The relief surging through was indescribable. To finally have this nightmare over with was a divine gift from heaven.

"Enjoy the rest of your honeymoon," she told the other woman. "Bessa and I owe you a real wedding gift as soon as you get back."

"I'm-a hold you to that, sugar."

Out in the hallway, Zeke placed the necklace carefully into the velvet pouch, then slipped it gently into his pocket.

Vivi released a pent-up sigh. "I can't believe something that fits in your pocket has caused us so much hassle."

"Hassle over, for the most part. Let's go. We should get dressed."

Vivi blinked up at him in confusion. Did he want to head back to Louisiana already? Of course, it made sense. Zeke Manning was a busy man. Now that he'd gotten what he came for, he had no more time to dally around staring at waterfalls with a café waitress who read tarot cards and did some singing on the side to make a living. As for that kiss, she'd read much more into it than she should have. A wave of disappointment waved over her heart and she silently chastised herself for it. How pathetic. Cute towns for honeymooners and aromatic rose gardens weren't her life. It was high time she got back to all that was.

"I won't be long," she said as they made their way to the elevator. "I don't have much to pack up. We can leave as soon as you'd like."

"Leave? Why would we do that?" He patted the pocket that held Esther's necklace. "Roxie and Rocky aren't the only ones who have something to celebrate tonight."

CHAPTER NINE

"You probably didn't pack anything too dressy, but there's a boutique a few doors down from the hotel," Zeke explained as they stepped into the lobby of their own hotel about fifteen minutes later. "While you shop, I'm going to get this to a safe-deposit box at the local bank until we can pick it up tomorrow."

Vivi could ascertain two things from what he'd just told her. One, they would be spending the night in Niagara Falls. Two, he planned to take her somewhere fancy, a place that required a dress from a boutique. The latter posed a bit of a problem, as she probably couldn't afford anything there.

Maybe if she maxed out her credit card. Who was she kidding? Even if she did take the hit, and run her card so high that she'd be paying it off for the next forty-eight to sixty months, her limit probably wouldn't even cover it.

Well, she'd figure out something. She was

good at that. Figuring out ways to adapt. She certainly wasn't about to admit to Zeke that her pocketbook precluded her from visiting any type of boutique. There had to be a discount store in the more touristy section of town. "How dressy are we talking?" she asked.

He must have read something in her voice, because he quickly added, "You can charge your purchases to my account. It's the least I can do for your aid in helping me get Esther's property back."

So they were back on this again. He was offering to compensate her once more. He really did view her as some kind of employee who'd simply helped him with a project. A man like Zeke would never view her as an equal. To him, she would always be from the wrong side of the tracks. He'd mentioned that it might surprise her how much he understood about the hardships she'd endured in her life. That may be so. But they weren't the same. Unlike her, Zeke had always had at least one person who'd wanted him. And he'd made something of himself. Whereas Vivi had to struggle every day just to get by. No wonder he saw her as nothing more than a temporary employee.

Which begged a major question—did he often go around kissing his employees?

Forget about the kiss. Zeke clearly had.

"That won't be necessary, Zeke. I wanted that necklace found as much as you did." If anything, she had a lot more riding on this quest they'd been on. Her reputation had hung on that necklace being returned to Esther. Maybe her very freedom.

To be returning to Louisiana with it safely in Zeke's possession really was the best-case scenario. She shuddered to think what might have happened if the authorities were involved. The last thing she needed was to have the law poking around in her life. Those days were long gone and she'd do all she could to ensure that they stayed safely behind.

"Vivi, I ins—" Zeke began before she cut him off with a palm up. He really didn't understand that she wasn't some charity case. Not for him, not for anyone. It was uncomfortable enough that he'd be paying for a restaurant that was sure to be pricey.

"It's not up for discussion," she said flatly, leaving him no room for further argument. "Just tell me what time to be ready."

He sighed with resignation but luckily didn't push any further. By now, they'd reached the door of their suite. "Let's meet back here in the common room in about three hours. Will that give you enough time?"

Vivi honestly didn't know. She was pretty certain this restaurant would be out of her league. The same way Zeke was out of her league. But she would make do with what she had to work with.

That was another thing she was good at.

Twenty minutes later Vivi put her resourcefulness to full use. The boutique Zeke mentioned was just as pricey as she'd imagined. But they had a rack of quality silk scarves that she could actually afford. Just barely.

She picked out one in a beautiful ocean-blue that she knew would bring out the specks of aqua in her eyes.

"Lovely choice," the young blonde at the register told her when she brought it up to be paid for and packaged.

"Thank you. It's about the only thing I can afford in here," she admitted. The clerk didn't seem like one of the pretentious ones so often employed in a place like this. Rather, she had a warm and pleasant smile that made Vivi feel at ease.

"The prices are outrageous," the other woman said with a mischievous smile, cupping her hand around her mouth as if divulging a state secret.

"Too high for me, I'm afraid. I was told to buy a fancy outfit for dinner tonight, but it won't be one of those." She gestured to the rack of beautiful gowns hanging along the wall. This was the kind of place that didn't even have visible price tags. She'd had to ask what the scarf sold for.

"Say no more." Vivi watched as the woman pulled out a slip of paper and started scribbling. She handed it to Vivi with a glance around the store to make sure no one was watching. The action struck Vivi as highly comical, seeing as they appeared to be the only two people in the store.

"Go there," she instructed, pointing to the sheet of paper. "They have the cutest outfits and they're always running discount sales. Not the best quality, but no one can tell."

That could be an apt description for a lot of things about her life, Vivi mused.

Zeke tucked the ticket for the safe-deposit box in the hotel room's safe and dialed the code to lock it. What a relief to know exactly where Esther's necklace was and that it was safe and secure.

He'd been less than certain more than once throughout the day that their efforts would be fruitful. Particularly when Vivi had been unable to provide Rocky's last name.

Luckily, it had somehow all worked out. Now he could relax and enjoy the evening. With Vivi. It was foolish of him to be so ardently looking forward to an evening out with her. But he figured they could both use it.

Without any kissing.

How in the world had he let that happen? He'd completely lost himself. She'd just looked so alluring in the garden, surrounded by flowers. And the way she sniffed the rose he'd given her, like a goddess bequeathed with a flower from heaven.

There he was waxing poetic again. He had to stop.

And it absolutely could not happen again. That much was certain.

As soon as he stepped into the common room to find Vivi waiting there, he realized just how much an effort it was going to take to stick to his resolutions.

She was absolutely stunning. Movie-star stunning. She wore a silky jumpsuit of some sort. Black material that somehow glittered navy blue when the light hit it a certain way. A sea-blue scarf hung low from her neck, and was tied in a complicated knot above her breastbone. Delicate tendrils of hair curled around her face. She wore that same red shade on her lips that had so vexed him that day in the French Quarter.

She did a mini twirl then spread her arms out. "What do you think? Will this work for where we're going?"

Think? Who could think? Not any warm-blooded male with eyes who caught sight of her. Clearing his throat, Zeke somehow managed to find voice enough to answer. "Yeah. That will work just fine."

The smile she gave at his response had his body tightening in all sorts of spots that had no business reacting in any way.

"Phew! I was worried a jumpsuit might not fit the bill."

"That one sure does," he mumbled.

Get a grip, already, buddy.

A beautiful woman shouldn't hamper his ability to speak coherently, for heaven's sake.

"Good. Because I'm starving."

Right. They should probably get a move on. While he was standing here on the verge of drooling at a woman he'd met only the day before, yet had already kissed, they were risking missing their reservation time. And the reservation had taken no small amount of string-pulling given that it had been made at the last minute.

"You mentioned you had your passport."

She nodded. "It's my primary form of ID. I don't drive. Why?"

"I figured we'd make this an international trip and head over to the Canadian side."

A dazzling smile appeared on her face and Zeke felt pleasure clear to his toes. The decision had been rather impulsive, but the look on Vivi's face told him he'd made the right call.

He held his elbow out to her. Vivi didn't hesitate before putting her hand on his arm and following him out the door.

The same driver that had picked them up at the airport was waiting for them outside and drove them through the border crossing into Ontario, Canada. They were at the restaurant moments later. The night had grown dark and the city was lit up at every turn. Just as many people roamed the streets as there had been this afternoon.

Vivi looked around her as they exited the car. A tall tower loomed several feet in front of them. The only structure in a square otherwise occupied by various vendors and street performers. "This is it? Where we're eating?" Her tone was one of curiosity and uncertainty. She had to be wondering if he'd had her get dressed up and cross the border to dine on another hot dog from a street cart.

"Sort of," he answered.

"What does that mean?" she asked, her eyes full of merriment. She was enjoying this. Knowing that made his heart do a little jump in his chest.

Zeke pointed up to the circular podlike structure at the top of the tower. "We'll be eating up there."

Her reaction was exactly as he'd hoped. She gasped out loud and clasped her free hand on her chest. "Oh, Zeke! I can't even imagine the view!"

"You won't have to imagine it. Let's go see it firsthand."

"I can hardly wait." She tugged on his arm, practically dragging him to the entrance.

"What a relief," he said on a chuckle. "I don't know what I would have done if you said you were afraid of heights." The statement was something of a fib. The thought had actually never crossed his mind. He'd known Vivi would be thrilled, that she wouldn't be bothered by the height one bit.

In fact, it was downright uncanny just how much he felt like he did know this woman.

Whatever winning a star meant in restaurant speak, this establishment deserved it. The place was opulent. Shiny silverware gleamed on crisp white tablecloths. The servers were all clad in tuxedos with starched, white-collared shirts and polished leather shoes.

But what Vivi really fixated on was the view. The entire city sat majestically before them, including the falls! She felt like a regal queen sitting atop her royal tower. And it was revolving! The scenery changed by the second. Food wasn't even necessary. She'd be perfectly content to just sit here and admire the scenery for hours.

She was so transfixed by the scene, she almost missed her chair when the server pulled it out for her to sit. Her bottom landed perilously close to the edge and she had to adjust herself to avoid toppling over.

You could take a girl to a fancy restaurant…

A waiter immediately appeared to fill their glasses with sparkling water. A different one showed up to hand them each thick leather-bound menus. Yet another came by after that and introduced himself as the sommelier. There appeared to be an entire team just to serve the two of them.

Zeke ordered a bottle of something Italian she couldn't pronounce while she looked over the menu. Just like the boutique, there didn't seem to be any prices listed anywhere.

If you have to ask the price, then you can't afford it.

She startled at Zeke's laughter, not realizing until that moment that she'd actually said the words out loud.

"Quite the quote," he commented.

"It's something one of my foster moms would say often. She used to watch those reality fashion makeover shows where the recipient always looked shocked when the overall cost of their transformation was revealed at the end."

Zeke's smile slowly waned. "One of your foster moms? How many houses were you sent to, exactly?"

She began a mental count before giving up. "About a dozen or so, I guess. I was a toddler when I entered the system, so I had time to bounce around before I aged out."

"That couldn't have been easy."

She shrugged. "Some houses were easier to leave than others. The toughest part was losing touch with some of the other kids. It was like repeatedly having to make friends only to never see them again once I left."

One girl in particular she still thought about often would always claim a spot in her heart. Lola. She'd been much younger. Vivi had felt more responsible for the child than their assigned mom. That's when Vivi's brushes with the law had first begun. But she didn't regret trying to help another child who'd needed it, and would probably do the same if she had to live it over again. The last time was a different story. She'd only been playing the fool for a man when that arrest had happened.

"It must have been a relief when you were able to leave," Zeke said, pulling her out of the unpleasant memories.

"It was and it wasn't. Then I had to figure out where to live and how to afford it. All on my own."

She knew she should try and change the subject. She was treading on very thin ice. One slipup and she'd be revealing more about herself than she wanted to. Zeke wasn't the type who would understand some of the things she'd done or why she'd had to do them. He would probably look at her the way some of those judges had over the years. Like she was lower than the tiled floor of the courthouse.

"Looks like you did just fine from where I'm standing."

It was silly, really. But the pleasure she felt at his compliment warmed her all over, from the top of her head right down to her toes.

"Thank you for that."

They grew silent as yet another tuxedoed server, female this time, appeared at their table with a bottle of wine. Uncorking it with expert skill and efficiency, she held it to Zeke, who sniffed then nodded approvingly. Vivi watched the ruby-red liquid pour into her glass, then Zeke's. The woman rested the bottle on a side table before walking away.

Several more moments went by in silence. Finally, Zeke spoke. "For what it's worth, I didn't exactly have what one would describe as a normal childhood, either."

Oh? That was surprising news. She would have pegged him as the type who'd lived in a perfectly tidy home surrounded by a picket fence and at least one, probably two, beloved household pets. Who'd had a set of adoring, attentive parents that exerted just the right amount of discipline without curbing their child's spirit. But that assessment wasn't a fair assumption now that she thought about it. She knew firsthand how deceiving looks could be.

He didn't elaborate further and Vivi was itching to ask but didn't want to push. Heaven knew she had things about her own past she wanted to keep close to her chest.

So she willed Zeke to continue, silently prodding him with a fixed gaze he didn't even seem to notice. She wanted to know everything about this enigmatic, charming man who swore too much and went out of his way to help little old ladies who'd carelessly given away their valuable antiques.

Probably best just to address the proverbial elephant in the room. She would take a guess and leave the ball in his court. "Parents' messy divorce?" she ventured.

He huffed out a humorless laugh. "Believe it or not, that would have been a blessing in comparison."

CHAPTER TEN

HE HADN'T MEANT to sound so cryptic. But what he'd said was the absolute truth. He and his sister would have preferred a messy, loud, battle-driven divorce to what their parents had put them through. His mother, to be more precise. His father had just been too weak to do anything to fix what was happening right in front of his nose. The man had been too cowardly to fight for his family, to protect his kids. A bitter surge of bile rose in his throat, almost ruining his appetite. He washed it away with the sparkling water, downing half the glass before setting it back down.

Vivi was looking at him expectantly. He had to give her something, he supposed. Fair was fair—she'd confided in him about her struggles as a foster child.

He waited while their salads arrived and more wine was poured in both their glasses. After taking a fortifying sip, he cleared his throat before beginning. Trying to put into words what he'd so carefully tucked away in a locked corner of his mind would take some effort. "In her attempt to live a more exciting and fulfilling life, my mother put her trust in the wrong person. People, to be more precise. It ended up costing us everything. We went from living a comfortable and affluent lifestyle to one of desperation and destitution." And filled with fear, he added silently. So much of his childhood had centered around the fear of one man and what he could get others to do for him.

Without a word, Vivi put down her salad fork and reached for his hand across the table. Her touch felt soft and comforting. Like the feeling of coming home after a long and arduous journey. He turned over his palm, taking her entire hand in his so they were clasped. To any outside observer, they probably appeared to be a besotted, loving couple out enjoying a special evening. For one insane moment, Zeke let himself pretend that was the reality. Several moments passed with them just holding each other's hands over the table. Almost as if they were a real couple.

Gently, he pulled his hand away and picked up his own fork. Vivi inhaled deeply before returning to her salad. "It's quite something, isn't it?" she asked.

"What is?"

"The complete and utter havoc others can wreak on our lives when we're not paying attention."

She was right but her words didn't really apply to him. He'd been paying attention, all right, as his world had slowly come crumbling down all those years ago. He'd just been too young and powerless to do anything about it.

Their head waiter appeared at their table to take their order. He opted for the night's special, a braised rack of lamb with fingerling potatoes. Vivi chose the sea bass, which was the chef's signature dish, they were told. Zeke took the liberty of ordering another bottle of wine. He wouldn't be driving anywhere, and the direction of their discussion seemed to warrant more liquid courage.

"Would your earlier statement have anything to do with your former tattoo?"

She chewed slowly, methodically, as if weighing her words. The guy must have done quite a number on her, since she couldn't even bring herself to talk about him.

An irrational and unexplainable anger swelled in his chest at the faceless, nameless man who'd clearly hurt Vivi so deeply that she still carried the wounds. What kind of fool would have let a woman like her go? She'd cared for tattoo guy enough to have his name engraved on her body in permanent ink. His ire began to turn to outrage the more he thought about it. Outrage that had nothing to do with jealousy. He just didn't like to see those who didn't deserve it get hurt. Maybe if he repeated that enough to himself, he'd eventually be convinced.

Finally, she spoke after a rather generous gulp of her wine. "It's a classic story, I suppose. Foolish, gullible girl trusts the wrong man. The repercussions of which follow her for years after. And probably will for the rest of her life."

So they'd both been burned by those who should have done better by them. Kindred spirits with respective painful memories they'd both rather forget.

A disquieting, uncomfortable feeling settled in his gut. This conversation had gotten too heavy, too personal. They were supposed to be two new friends enjoying the successful resolution of a rather stressful matter that they no longer needed to worry about. The mood at the table right now was anything but celebratory. He was racking his brain for a way to fix that when the universe did it for him.

As if on cue, the wall of glass in front of them revolved so they had a perfect view of the falls. Just then illuminative lights went on. The entirety of the falls turned into a massive kaleidoscope. It was a spectacular display of lights and color and rushing water. Like something out of a brilliant painting. Only the art here happened to be vibrantly changing and moving.

Vivi's gasp was audible. "Oh, my," she said on a breathless sigh. "Would you look at that."

But he wasn't watching the display of lights that had taken her breath away. He couldn't take his eyes off *her*. Her breathing was heavy and quick, at a near pant. The excitement was practically buzzing from her as she stared at the stunning light-and-laser display in wonder and amazement. She was mesmerized.

And so was Zeke. But that had nothing to do with the view from their table.

He was falling for her. Sometime over the last couple of days, his feelings toward Vivi had gone from mere attraction to affection. An affection he had to fight. For a woman like Vivi could ruin him if he let her. Like Vivi said, he could really get burned if he wasn't paying enough attention.

Vivi reluctantly pushed away her plate after taking one last scrumptious bite. The meal was a culinary masterpiece, every morsel delivering a burst of flavor on her tongue. Very likely the tastiest meal she'd ever had—and she lived in New Orleans, one of the food capitals of the world. But she couldn't eat any more. Her tummy was resoundingly, soundly stuffed. It had taken years, but she'd finally taught herself to stop eating when she was full. Before that, it had felt like such a waste to let any food go uneaten considering how many nights she'd gone to bed hungry.

"Dessert?" Zeke asked, pulling her out of the memories. There'd certainly been a lot of those unearthed this evening. She wasn't quite sure how she felt about that. Somehow she'd managed to keep most of her past buried while still confiding in Zeke to some degree.

"I can't eat another bite," she replied, tapping her middle.

"I say we walk a bit and enjoy the night air. You game?"

She definitely was. A walk in the fresh air might help clear her head. "Definitely."

No bill had arrived for their meal, but Zeke stood and walked over to assist her out of her chair. All their waiters nodded politely as they left the table, and no one gave chase when they made it to the elevator. Vivi concluded that payment had probably been arranged beforehand.

The rich certainly lived differently than the rest of the world.

When they left the tower, the square outside was just as busy as when they'd arrived earlier this evening. If anything, it appeared even more crowded. A band had set up in the center, playing instrumental versions of current top-forty popular hits. Several people were dancing in front. Vivi had to hop out of the way of one couple doing some kind of complicated tango.

She suddenly felt a strong hand on her shoulder. Zeke gently turned her to face him. "Care for a dance?" He held his hand out, palm up. Vivi took it and stepped closer. With a chuckle, he took her in his arms and together they began to move to the beat. He'd undone the top button of his dress shirt, revealing a tanned triangle of skin. She itched to touch him there, imagined trailing her fingers from the base of his neck down lower, to where a small sprinkle of chest hair peeked out from under his shirt. The aftershave she'd grown so fond of tickled her nose and she inhaled deeply, trying to get her fill.

She looked up to catch him staring at her. Something shifted in the air between them. Though the music remained up-tempo and bouncy, Zeke pulled her closer and slowed his steps, his arms tight around her waist. She could feel his hot breath on her cheek, his pulse pound under her palm. Was he going to kiss her again? Dear heavens, she wanted him to. She really, really wanted it.

The tangoing couple barreled into them in

that instant. Vivi felt herself falling into Zeke's body, sandwiched between the couple and his chest. Somehow he kept his balance despite the three people crashing into him.

The other gentleman straightened and gave them an apologetic smile. *"Excusez nous."*

Zeke answered the man in French, then proceeded to have a brief conversation with the couple in the other language. He was clearly fluent. Was there any talent the man didn't have?

"You're bilingual," she said as the other couple moved on.

He still held her in his arms. "Trilingual, actually," he answered without any hint of grandeur. "I do a lot of business in Europe. Particularly France." He tilted his head toward the other couple, who were still tangoing despite the change to a slower song. Something told her they'd indulged in some liquid courage as well at some point. "Though their dialect was a little different than what I'm used to as they're French Canadian."

"What other language are you fluent in?"

"Just Italian and French," he answered. Vivi had to chuckle at the *just*.

"It was easier to learn the languages seeing as I'm in those countries so often. In fact, I'm due in Provence in a couple of days."

The comment brought Vivi hurling back to

reality. This was all fun and games, dining with Zeke Manning. Dancing with him outside while an amateur band played cheerful music. But she couldn't forget how unreal all this was. How temporary. Fantasyland would come crashing to an end in about forty-eight short hours. Zeke would leave for France and leave her life. Probably never to think of her again.

She suddenly didn't feel like dancing anymore.

"I think I'm ready to move on," she told him, stepping out of his embrace. He let her go, but stopped her with a hand on her arm after a few steps.

"Let's go a bit further before returning to the car."

She followed him away from the partying dancers and out of the square. It only took a few steps for her to determine they were headed back in the direction of the falls. The prospect of visiting it again lifted her spirits somewhat. But not by much. She'd never be able to forget Zeke Manning. Would wonder every day where he was and what he was doing.

How had this happened? She'd fallen for him. And she hadn't even seen it coming. She'd been caught completely unaware.

"Thank you," she said a few minutes later as the sound of the falls grew louder the closer they came.

"You already thanked me for dinner."

"Now I'm thanking you for bringing me back to see the water."

He gave a small shrug. "I promised you we'd go back. What kind of man doesn't keep a promise to his almost-wife?"

Zeke regretted the words as soon as they left his mouth. He really had no business calling Vivi any kind of wife. Not even jokingly. They were simply two people enjoying some time together before they had to go their separate ways. And he and Vivi absolutely had to go their separate ways, being from different worlds that could never collide in any kind of positive way. They both had way too much baggage. And the bags he had were much too heavy to burden anyone else with.

Vivi deserved better.

Now his words hung heavy between them, too late to take them back.

"You shouldn't say such things to me," Vivi told him, confirming his regret. "Calling me a wife implies permanence." She motioned around her. "None of this is permanent. By this time tomorrow I'll be back in New Orleans and you'll be getting ready to fly to another continent."

Heaven help him, that last sentence came out on a sob. He'd never meant for her to become so emotionally invested, wasn't even sure how or when it had happened. He would have to do better. He wanted to get closer to her, to hold her and comfort her. But touching her was the last thing either of them needed.

"You're right. I was careless. It won't happen again."

"No?"

He shook his head. "No."

She visibly swallowed. "And what about earlier today? With what happened in the rose garden."

Right. Their kiss. He should have known that would come up. Yet another transgression to apologize for.

"That won't happen again, either. Consider it another promise."

The color of the lights illuminating the falls changed right then. They went from neon rainbow colors to a combination of soft reds and ambers. The hues brought out the warm hue of Vivi's eyes, and there was no missing the moisture in them.

Her tongue darted out to lick her lips. People strolled by them—all around them the world continued on. But they may as well have been the only people on earth. Nothing mattered now but the woman in front of him and what she was telling him.

"What if I don't want you to make that promise?"

Zeke's breath caught in his throat. Had he heard her correctly? "Vivi, what exactly are you saying? I need to be certain here."

She stepped closer to him, then tilted her head up to his. "I'm asking you to kiss me again, Zeke."

Zeke felt his mouth go dry, his heart beat like a bass drum in his chest. He wouldn't make her ask twice.

His mouth was on hers in the next instant. Vivi wrapped her arms around his neck and held tight. He couldn't get enough of her. And when she ran her tongue along his lower lip, he thought he might collapse from the sheer pleasure.

A low groan vibrated against his mouth. He wasn't even sure which one of them it had come from. Finally, Vivi was the first one to pull away. He felt her loss as if a bucket of cold water had been thrown at him.

She stood before him, breathless and panting, and it took all he had not to drag her back into his arms and repeat what had just happened.

Heaven help him, but he wanted more. Much more.

It was impossible to sleep. Zeke gripped the cold metal bar of the hotel suite balcony railing and watched the lights of the city below gradually go out one by one. He'd lost track of how long he'd been standing there when only a handful of shops' lights remained lit. The town was slowly going to sleep.

Unlike him. Insomnia had cursed him for close to two hours until he'd finally admitted defeat and come out here for some fresh air. He couldn't get that kiss out of his mind. Either kiss.

The way Vivi had tasted, how she'd felt in his arms. The vulnerability on her face as she'd so boldly asked for what she wanted. It all ran in a continuous loop in his mind. The fact that their time together was coming to an end was affecting him more than it should have.

He had no idea what he was going to do about it.

She didn't realize, of course, but he'd never so much as spoken about his past with anyone who wasn't his sister. And his only sibling preferred to avoid the topic of their shared trauma even more than he did.

Somehow, Vivi had pushed through defenses he hadn't even acknowledged he'd built around himself. He couldn't even pinpoint when it had happened. She visited old ladies and didn't charge them for readings. She elicited fierce loyalty from those who seemed to know her the best. She listened without judgment or expectation.

Zeke hadn't realized just how much he'd wanted that from someone until it was right there in front of him in the form of one Vivienne Ducarne.

Zeke rubbed a hand down his face and grabbed the icy bottle of water he'd brought out with him, emptying it in a few quick gulps. The rich dinner and all the wine had left him parched.

He turned to go back inside for another bottle from the mini fridge when the balcony door suddenly swung open and Vivi stepped outside. She startled when she saw him. In a spaghetti-strap tank and boy shorts that showed off her shapely legs, she looked better than any woman should at this time of night.

"Sorry, I didn't realize you were out here. I'll go back in. You probably want to be alone."

Before she could turn away, he reached for her, gently taking her by the shoulder. "Vivi, stay. I'm just getting some air."

She hesitated for the briefest of seconds before slowly shutting the door and reaching for one of the lounge chairs.

"You couldn't sleep, either, huh?" he asked as she sat down with a thump.

"Been tossing and turning since I crawled into bed an hour ago."

He could certainly relate. They were both probably preoccupied by the same thoughts. "Ditto."

Maybe neither of them wanted the night to end, considering they'd both be returning to their ordinary lives tomorrow. Or later today to be more accurate. It was already almost two thirty in the morning.

Damn it. He had a nice life to go back to. He'd worked hard to get to where he was after burying his tumultuous past. He had no business begrudging it in any way. Even if his time in France in a few days would involve thwarting the unwanted advances of a lonely former winery owner.

But there was no denying that the thought of going back to normal held zero appeal at the moment.

And that feeling had everything to do with the woman sitting in front of him.

She'd said while they'd been walking after dinner that whatever was happening between them wasn't permanent. Was that so wrong? What exactly was so wrong with temporary, anyway?

"Come to France with me, Vivi."

She jerked her head up in shock. Well, he

was pretty surprised himself. He had no idea he'd intended to utter those words until they'd left his mouth.

Vivi stood staring at him, slack-jawed. He scrambled for a way to continue. "You'd be doing me a favor."

"A favor? How?"

"My clients in France are a rather traditional family. They think I'd make a perfect match for their single daughter. They've tried several times in the past to set me up with her."

She blinked in confusion. Of course she was confused. He was making a mighty mess of this. How many times could he behave so uncharacteristically unprepared around this woman.

"I see," she simply said.

"It gets distracting and uncomfortable. I'm only there on business and don't need the added complication of fending off such requests," Zeke explained, hoping he was making some kind of sense.

"What has that got to do with me going to France with you?" Vivi asked.

He shrugged. "Simple. It might help if they think I'm already involved with someone. I figure we can pretend to be a couple."

CHAPTER ELEVEN

Two days later

"TALK ME OUT of this before I do something I'm going to regret, Bessa."

Vivi paused in the act of packing when her roommate walked into her bedroom.

"I'll do no such thing. I think you should go for it. I just came in here to offer you these." She held out a plate of steaming hot hush puppies. "I just made them fresh."

Bessa was known in the neighborhood for her hush-puppy recipe, one she kept secret even from the woman she'd shared an apartment with for the last three years. Vivi reached for one and tossed it from one hand to the other as the ball of fried dough burned her palms.

"Careful, they're hot."

"Fried dough isn't the only way a girl could get burned, you know."

As far as metaphors went, it was kind of lame.

But it pretty much captured the way Vivi felt about her decision to say yes the other night on the hotel balcony. Like she'd been impulsive and might be risking irreparable harm to herself.

Mainly to her heart.

Zeke had completely shocked her when he'd asked her to accompany him on his trip to France. She knew she should have given it more thought. But the idea of being able to spend more time with him, in a setting as romantic as the French countryside, had been too tempting to ignore. She simply hadn't the will to turn him down, though that would have been the wisest move. Hindsight, as they said.

"Huh," Bessa responded, taking a bit of one of her creations and plopping down on Vivi's bed while she chewed. "Some fires are worth getting close to."

Vivi wasn't so sure about that theory. Look how badly her relationship with Todd had scarred her. Not that it made any kind of sense to compare the two men. Zeke was everything Todd could ever hope to be. Smart, eloquent. Someone who knew how to treat a woman.

Oh, and Zeke didn't have a rap sheet the length of a swamp gator.

"Said the unsuspecting moth right before his wings were singed," Vivi answered, folding another pair of jeans and tossing them in her bag. She was apparently full of bad metaphors today.

"How did this come about, anyway?" Bessa asked. "He just out and asked you to fly to France with him."

That was exactly what had happened. "Yes," she answered Bessa simply.

"You two must have really hit it off."

That was one way to describe it. "He said the client he deals with in France always tries to hit on him. To the point where it's gotten awkward for a professional such as himself," Vivi explained. "So bringing me along when he goes to their estate might cool her jets a bit."

Bessa barked out a sharp laugh. "He wants you to pretend to be his girlfriend? I'm thinking there won't be much pretense needed."

"It's not like that," Vivi lied, recalling the way he'd kissed her by the falls. How his mouth on hers had melted her insides. Even thinking about it now had her knees nearly buckling.

"So what happened when you told him about…you know?"

Realization dawned on Bessa's features at Vivi's continued silence to her question.

"Oh," Bessa finally said, not needing an actual answer anymore.

"I probably should have. And maybe I will on this trip. But there never seemed to be the right time in Niagara Falls. Especially not during the time a valuable necklace had gone missing."

"I see your point."

Vivi sighed and checked her purse yet again to ensure her passport was there. Not being a driver, she relied on it as her primary form of identification. Which had certainly come in handy when a man she'd met just last week had taken her into another country then asked her to fly to Europe with him.

Another wave of doubt flushed through her center. "Maybe I should call off the whole thing. Tell him I can't go after all."

Bessa popped a whole hush puppy in her mouth. "Isn't it kind of late?" she asked between bites. "You said he's due to pick you up at three. It's one thirty now."

Bessa had a point. It would be unfair to cancel on Zeke at the last minute. Why was she overthinking it, anyway? He wanted her to help him out with an overflirtatious client. It just so happened that she'd be helping him in one of the most romantic and awe-inspiring spots on earth.

Bessa seemed to read her thoughts. "Why don't you just go and enjoy yourself. Leave all the worrying for when you get back. This is a dream vacation to Europe and you're thinking about passing it up."

She was right. There'd be plenty of time to regret her decision later. When the trip was long over and Zeke was back in New York, and she didn't know if or when she'd ever see him again, no doubt the mighty beast of regret would rear its head. Vivi happened to do regret really well. But at least this time, she'd have a visit to France to remember.

"You might be right."

"I always am. As for the rest, wouldn't you rest easier if you just confided in him? Just told him what happened in the past and explained it wasn't really your fault."

Vivi stepped over to the bed and gave her friend a tight hug. Bessa was usually spot-on. But not this time. Not about this. Zeke would never understand that her ex-boyfriend had duped her into waiting in a getaway car while he committed armed robbery inside a pawnshop. That fateful day was the reason she still couldn't bring herself to sit behind the wheel of a car.

And he certainly wouldn't understand that she'd done a short stint in juvie simply because she'd wanted to make sure a younger child had clothes on her back and enough food to eat.

He probably wouldn't even listen to her version of events. The same way the cops, lawyers and judges hadn't listened.

* * *

Bessa's description had been an apt one. Vivi really felt as if she might be in some kind of daydream the next day as she sat in a rental sports car—a cabriolet—with Zeke in the driver's seat. He maneuvered the car expertly along cliffside curves and the French countryside while Vivi admired the view. Now that she was here, she couldn't believe she'd almost turned down the opportunity. She may live to regret her decision, but for now she was going to enjoy every moment she could.

Like her roommate had also said, "Deal with the worrying when you get back." Wise woman, that Bessa was. Most of the time.

They were headed to meet the winery owners to finalize the sale to Zeke's American corporate client.

"We shouldn't be there long," he told her now over the wind. "Once I get the paperwork signed and sealed, we can take some time to sightsee."

"That sounds wonderful," she shouted so that he could hear her, then laughed at how comically loud she'd just sounded.

Zeke responded with a grin in her direction before turning his attention back to the road. "What's so funny?"

"Nothing, really. I'm just having a really good time so far." Which made almost no sense, as they'd only been in the country a short while after having landed at Marseille Provence Airport earlier today.

"Not too jet-lagged?"

"Not at all." That was the truth. Rather, she felt energized and ready for the adventures that lay ahead while they were here. She'd never been to an authentic winery or a lavender field before. Let alone done those things in the south of France.

Several minutes later they turned onto a dusty dirt road surrounded by the greenest grass she'd ever seen. The smell of the sea permeated the air. When the house appeared in front of them a few moments later, Vivi had to suck in a breath. It looked like something out of one of those foreign dubbed movies Bessa made her go to occasionally. A sprawling mansion with a tall, round center building flanked by a wing on each side. Behind the structure she could see the rows and rows of lush grapevines on a rising hill.

"Welcome to the Château de Seville," Zeke said as he put the car in Park and killed the ignition. "I know I thanked you earlier, but I'm doing so again."

"You've flown me to France and our first stop is a gorgeous château. I'm the one who should be thanking you, Zeke."

"You're doing me a favor, remember? This

visit will go much quicker and much smoother if I don't have to keep finding creative ways to turn down Michelline's offer of a romantic dinner over and over."

Vivi had to feel for the other woman she hadn't met yet. She understood firsthand how easy it was to fall for Zeke Manning. A small, foolish part of her wished there didn't need to be any pretense. And that she really was here as Zeke's partner. But she was nothing more than a decoy. A fake.

This Michelline couldn't know, but the two of them had a lot in common—pining for the same man who didn't feel the same about them as they felt about him.

Sisters in spirit, Vivi thought as she followed Zeke up the pathway to the large wooden door of the main building. It flung open as soon as Zeke knocked. An older, rotund woman stood on the other side. She greeted them with a warm smile, though the smile directed in Vivi's direction faltered ever so slightly.

"Madame Seville, *bonjour,*" Zeke began, then continued with a slew of more French words Vivi didn't have a hope of understanding. He motioned to her with his hand and said her name.

The other woman took Vivi's hand and shook it just as her husband appeared at the door. She said something to her directly in French. "She wants to apologize for speaking a language you can't understand," Zeke explained, translating.

Within minutes the four of them were seated around a rustic wooden table enjoying wine and a platter of various cheeses and dried fruits.

Zeke stuck to mostly water, since he was driving.

Vivi could only nod and smile politely, having no clue what was transpiring around her. Occasionally, Zeke threw her an indulgent smile.

The Seville home was cozy and comfortably decorated, despite being an official château. Pens were pulled and mounds of papers were signed.

Michelline had still not made an appearance.

A twinge of guilt settled in Vivi's middle. She knew Zeke had his reasons for this charade. And this family really had put him in an awkward spot if they consistently tried to set him up with their daughter. Still, she couldn't help but feel sympathy toward the other woman. She was in a rather similar situation, wasn't she?

Finally, Zeke began to pack up all the paperwork and slid it back into his leather carrying case. He stood and shook the hands of their hosts. The scene served to alleviate Vivi's guilt somewhat—clearly there were no hard feelings and from what little she could tell of the conversation, the Sevilles had made quite a bit of a profit on the sale of their estate. Monsieur Seville even gifted Zeke a bottle of their special reserve from the previous harvest as a token of thanks.

They were headed to the door to leave when a tall, elegantly dressed woman turned the corner from the hallway. Vivi could only stare in stunned silence. She had to be the mysterious Michelline.

Whatever Vivi had been expecting, it didn't compare to the woman who stood before them with a friendly yet tight smile. She looked like something out of a fashion spread in a magazine. Rich honey-blond hair fell in waves over her elegant bare shoulders. She was dressed in a strapless dress that hugged her delicate curves just so. Her nails had been perfectly manicured, including the ones on her toes.

This was the woman that Zeke was trying to avoid?

"Zeke," she began, and her thick French accent made his simple name sound regal and exotic. "So lovely to see you. And you have brought a guest." She clasped Vivi's hand in hers then air-kissed both her cheeks.

"Th-thank you," Vivi stammered. The woman was clearly fluent in English but Vivi had no idea what else to say.

"Michelline, we missed you during the signing," Zeke said, smiling in return.

"It is done, then?" Michelline asked.

"*Oui*. Your parents can live comfortably the rest of their lives without worrying about the demands of running and upkeep of a successful winery."

"We have you to thank for that, don't we?" Michelline said with clear gratitude, then she turned back to Vivi. "You know, despite the fact that he works for the other party, Zeke convinced our buyers to up their offer and sweeten the deal on behalf of Mama and Papa."

"Wow" was all Vivi could manage to say. She wasn't surprised by what Michelline had just said. She hadn't known him long, but she knew Zeke would fight for the underdog no matter what side he was technically on.

It was one of the many things that had her falling for him.

And she was falling for him—there was no denying it any longer. Somehow along the way, in the span of a few short days, Vivi had gone from attraction to admiration to something much more.

Rather inconvenient.

She studied Zeke's profile now as they drove away from the Seville home. His hair was a windblown mess, but somehow on him it looked rugged and masculine. He'd taken off his jacket and rolled up his shirtsleeves about the elbow.

Her heart did a little flutter in her chest and she made herself look away before he could see the longing in her eyes.

"Ready to tour those lavender fields now?" he asked her, pulling her out of her thoughts.

"I'm looking forward to it."

"It's about a half-hour ride from here," he informed her.

Before even half that amount of time passed, it was clear that fate had other plans. A massive storm cloud appeared in the sky, churning and angry. Vivi ducked her head to get a better look. Not good. It seemed to go on for miles and miles in the sky.

"What in the hell?" Zeke groaned. "There was no thunderstorm or any kind of weather event in the forecast. It's supposed to be a sunny and clear day."

The fact that he'd made sure to check the weather forecast before setting up a plan to take her to a lavender field seemed so true to his character. Zeke Manning didn't seem to like leaving anything to chance. But meticulous planning only went so far at times. Times like right now, for instance.

Vivi pointed up. "I don't think Mr. Cloud up there cares what the meteorologists predicted."

Zeke frowned and hit the button to pull up the cover on the convertible. It closed just in the nick of time. A sheet of heavy rain dropped like a waterfall from the sky. It reminded her of the Horseshoe Falls back in Niagara Falls. Only now it felt like they might be standing right under it.

Zeke slowed the car to a crawl. "I can't see a thing. And it doesn't look like it's going to let up anytime soon."

Before he even got the last word out, a flash of lightning lit up the air around them, as if someone had flipped on a massive light switch then shut it right back off. The following thunder noticeably shook the small car. Zeke pulled out his phone. His lips tightened as he clicked on an icon on the screen and studied what loaded up.

"This doesn't look good," he announced.

She could have surmised that from the messy conditions outside, as well as the concerned look on his face.

Another bolt of lightning struck through the air, this one perilously close to where they were, followed by thunder so loud it made Vivi jump in her seat. The sky grew so dark it may as well have been nightfall. How had all this come about so quickly and without any kind of warning?

Vivi was no stranger to rough weather. She lived in New Orleans, for Pete's sake, where the seasonal hurricanes had devastated the city in previous years. But right now they were in the middle of nowhere, completely isolated.

"We need to find shelter," he told her, putting the car back in gear and moving slowly. The wipers may as well not have been running. They weren't helping in any way to be able to see out the windshield.

"Is there anything out here even?" Visibility was zero at the moment, but they'd been driving for miles before the cloud appeared and there had been nothing but fields and greenery.

"According to my map icon, there's a structure up ahead."

Vivi didn't like the word he'd just used. What did he mean by *structure*? Why didn't he say *cottage*? Or *pub*? She took out her own phone to see for herself what was nearby. The no-signal warning greeted her when she clicked the button. Icy dread ran up her spine. If they needed help, there'd be no way to call for it.

"We just lost cell reception," she informed Zeke.

"Not surprising. If we could just get to this building and get a roof over our heads."

"What kind of structure are we talking about?"

The road they were on was steadily flooding

now and Vivi could feel the vehicle actually hydroplane underneath them.

Zeke released a deep breath, his fingers in a death grip on the steering wheel. "It appears to be an abandoned château."

CHAPTER TWELVE

ZEKE WANTED TO kick himself for putting Vivi in such a harrowing situation. That she was in any kind of peril because of his decisions made him feel like an absolute heel. In his defense, the storm seemed to have come out of nowhere. Even the weather reports hadn't seen it coming.

At least he'd found them some shelter. Even if it was in the form of a damp, dusty and moldy abandoned brick mansion that probably hadn't seen any human activity in years, aside from the occasional squatter.

He handed Vivi his jacket from the back seat of the car. "Here. Cover your head. We're both going to get soaked, anyway, but it's something, at least."

She didn't protest, but took it from him with a quick thanks. Luckily he'd thrown their carry-on bags in the back seat as opposed to the trunk. He grabbed them both in one hand and braced himself. The château was only a few feet away, but in this mess it was going to be a harrowing jaunt.

"Ready?" he asked Vivi.

Her lips were tight, her eyes apprehensive, as she nodded. "As ready as I'm gonna get."

"On the count of three."

He hadn't even gotten to one before she threw open her door and leaped outside.

Zeke watched in admiration as she ran to the gaping hole in the front of the building that had once been a front door. Way to rip off the bandage without any preamble or hesitation. Why had he expected anything less from her?

She disappeared into the building and he rushed to her side. They were both soaked to the skin in just the few seconds it had taken to make it from the car.

He'd been right about the state of the building. Cobwebs hung from the high ceiling. Moldy grime clung to the walls. Several wooden beams were strewn about. But it appeared sound and steady. And it was a roof over their heads in a storm.

He turned to see Vivi shivering with cold. Her hair was wet and plastered to her head. Her clothing a soaked, disheveled mess.

She looked absolutely adorable.

How did a woman manage to look so sexy shivering and soaking wet?

"Hope we're not here long," she commented, studying the dank and dark space. "Not that I'm not grateful to be out of that tin can of a car." She paused, then added, "No offense."

"None taken. It's a rental."

A harsh gust of wind brought some of the rain through the open doorway and they moved farther inside. Zeke dropped the bags he was carrying on the floor and unzipped the one that belonged to him. Reaching inside, he pulled out one of his long-sleeved T-shirts and a gym towel he always carried in the side compartment with his toiletries. He handed the latter to Vivi.

"It's small, but it's absorbent."

"Thanks."

She did her best to dry off and the shivering seemed to abate if only a little. He handed her the shirt. "Here. Something dry."

He turned around so she could change, but not before he could stop the images from flooding his mind. Images of him helping her to take off her wet top, running his hand down her rib cage and over her lips. Pulling her tight against him.

Steady, there. The lady was just trying to get warm and dry.

A few moments later, he heard her clear her throat. "All set. Thanks. That's much better."

The shirt was about three sizes too big for her, and hung like a curtain off her shoulders with the sleeves draped down past her hands. Again, somehow she made it look fetching. In fact, he itched to take her in his arms and devour those damp lips until she was shivering again, but this time for all the right reasons.

He clenched his fists at his side instead. He yanked out another dry shirt, then peeled off the wet one and tossed it aside. As soaked as it was, the Italian silk was most likely ruined, anyway. He pulled the dry one over his chest and torso. Vivi made a deliberate show of looking down at her toes until he was done.

"Well, we could be here for a while," he said, studying the layout of the place to see what they had to work with. "May as well make ourselves comfortable."

Vivi looked around. "How, exactly, do you propose we do that?"

He reached inside his bag again, and found the wine Monsieur Seville had given him just a short time ago. "This should help."

"Merci, Monsieur Seville," she said with a smile.

Zeke unzipped the side pocket and pulled out the granola bar he kept there for nights when he didn't have time to grab a real dinner. "And there's this."

"Resourceful. I'm impressed."

"Tonight, we feast."

"Only one problem." She pointed to the bottle he held. "How do we get that open?"

Like a cartoon, Zeke literally scratched his head in concentration, earning a hearty chuckle from Vivi.

"I saw someone online use a key once to twist off a cork," she offered.

"Worth a try, I guess." Zeke yanked the car-key fob out his pocket and clicked it open to remove the metal key inside.

Twenty minutes and several attempts later, he finally managed to pull out the cork, though some of it had broken apart and fallen into the bottle. Vivi cheered and clapped at his success and he gave her a small bow. "Now we can finally feast."

"Let's see if we can find a dry corner somewhere." When they did, Vivi set down her travel blanket on the ground and they both did their best to fit on it together. Her shoulder and hip rubbed tight against his side as they took turns biting the granola bar and taking sips straight from the bottle.

Warmth spread along his skin everywhere her body touched his. She smelled of fruity shampoo and damp skin. His fingers itched to run his touch over her shoulders and down her arms, and he longed to taste the wine on her lips. Somehow, he made himself resist the urge to pull her closer against him. This wasn't the time or place. They were caught in a raging rainstorm, for heaven's sake.

A storm that showed no signs of letting up. In fact, it seemed to have only grown stronger and more formidable outside. But Zeke found he didn't really mind. He was in no hurry to leave.

If someone had told her a month ago that she'd be huddled up in the corner of an abandoned castle in the French countryside eating a granola bar and drinking wine straight out of the bottle with a man she'd recently met, Vivi would have laughed until her stomach hurt.

Her life had been a series of unexpected twists since Zeke had arrived in it. Had it really been only a number of days since Zeke had stormed into the magic shop demanding to know where Esther's necklace was? It seemed like it had happened months ago.

Even their visit to the winery felt like it had occurred sometime in the distant past rather than just a short while ago. Every minute with Zeke Manning seemed to pack a myriad of experiences.

She recalled what Michelline had said about Zeke making sure her parents got the best deal they could from his client.

"That was very noble of you," she said to him

now. In her desire to get warm using his heat, she'd given up fighting the urge to snuggle into his warm chest, her back against his front with his arms around her. Who was she kidding? It felt nice to be snuggled up against him, to feel his rock-hard chest against her back. If she was being fanciful, she might have said they fit together well.

"Noble?" he asked.

"How you made sure to take care of the Sevilles rather than try to shortchange them in any way on behalf of your client."

"My client is a conglomerate of successful wineries throughout the world. The Sevilles ran a family winery and worked hard their whole lives to make it succeed. It was easy to make sure they were given their due."

He was trying to minimize it, but not many attorneys would have even taken such factors into consideration, let alone work to ensure fair play. No lawyer she'd ever had the misfortune to deal with would ever have gone to any such trouble. Even the ones whose job was to defend her couldn't wait to rush to a plea then wash their hands of her. Zeke was a rarity indeed from what she'd encountered throughout her life.

"What you did for them was commendable, Zeke. So was making sure Esther got her necklace back."

He nuzzled the top of her head with his chin. "Any other attorney would have probably done the same in both cases."

That wasn't true and he had to know it. "Why?" she asked simply, counting on him understanding exactly what she was asking.

He was silent for so long that she thought he might not answer. "I don't like seeing people taken advantage of," he finally responded.

Vivi didn't want to push. But she was so curious about what made him tick. How had Zeke Manning become the man that he was today? Maybe it was the wine. It seemed to be going to her head with nothing but half a granola bar to soak up what she drank, but she found herself asking the questions that were running through her mind. "You said your family went from comfort to destitution. What happened to cause that, Zeke. May I ask?"

His arms tightened around her waist. "It didn't happen all at once. My mother was the type who was always bored. Always needed to feel excited about something."

That sounded like a pretty exhausting way to grow up. Vivi didn't voice the thought out loud, just remained silent to allow Zeke the chance to share what he wanted to share. Or to end the discussion if he wanted to.

He went on, "She held these grand parties at

our house. Hosted artists and singers and writers. She considered herself a grand patron of true talent. Certain she was about to discover the next best thing."

Vivi felt him take a deep breath behind her before continuing. "All the while, my dad just did what he had to do to make sure we could afford it all. He worked for a major law firm and invested well, but eventually it wasn't enough. Not after my mom met an up-and-coming painter. Rex Waltham. He had my mother convinced he was the next Andy Warhol. She bought everything he painted or drew."

Vivi could just guess where this was going. And it broke her heart. "Eventually, Rex moved in. I actually had to give up my room so he could stay there with us. At the awkward age of thirteen I had to share a room with my younger sister. And my father didn't do anything about it. Just continued to bring in the money to keep my mother happy. He wasn't a strong man. Too weak to fight and too complacent. It was easier to just try and indulge her. And my old man always took the easy way out."

"But it wasn't enough," he added after a pause. "It was never enough."

The pieces that made up the puzzle that was Zeke Manning started to slowly fall in place. His protectiveness and fierce desire to ensure fairness. His lack of trust and propensity to think the worst of others. The way he had about *her*.

"That man used her and spit her out," he said after another long pause. "He finally left after finding the next, much richer mark. But by then it was too late. My father was a shell of his former self. Sick and weak. He wasn't with us long after that."

Tears stung her eyes at the pain in his voice. He'd been so young. To have his whole life turned upside down by those who should have loved him enough to protect him. "You must have been so strong. To just even survive that."

He grunted out an unamused laugh. "I had to do more than survive. After my dad was gone, I had to pick up all the pieces. Make sure my mother got help for her issues and that my younger sister was taken care of."

"What did you do?"

"As soon as I was old enough, I worked for anyone who would hire me. My sister and I ended up moving in with my grandmother. All four of us crammed into a tiny condo in Brunswick. At that point our house had been taken. An unoriginal McMansion, but it had been home. Then one day it was just gone. Any savings or investment was already long spent. Rex somehow convinced my mother to keep investing in him until there was nothing left."

She felt his muscles stiffen behind her. His heart was beating like a drum against her back.

"I somehow managed to put myself through college and then law school. Last I heard, my mother had traveled out to the West Coast, living in some kind of co-op or commune. None of us have heard from her in years."

Vivi let everything he'd just told her sink in. She'd thought he was accomplished before. She'd had no idea. Just thinking about all he'd had to overcome just to survive. But he'd gone on to do so much more than that.

One thing was for certain—Zeke had been taught from an early age that trust was never to be given lightly. How could she ever expect him to trust someone like her if he ever found out the truth?

Amazingly, they'd both fallen sleep. It was the cramping pain below the back of his skull that woke him up. Zeke stirred and tried to roll out the kink in his neck muscles. Sleeping against a hard stone wall while sitting upright was not ideal for a man his size or age.

The wine bottle sat empty by his right thigh. The granola-bar wrapper was crumpled up on Vivi's lap.

A small ray of sunshine shone through one of the square window holes on the second floor,

casting light on the ground next to his feet. And
it was quiet. No thunder, no steady beat of rain-
fall. The storm seemed to have passed.

What time was it?

Zeke tried to lift his arm to peek at his watch,
but he couldn't quite move with Vivi sprawled
on top of him. They'd been sitting next to each
other against the wall, but at some point she'd
ended up square in his lap. Not that he was com-
plaining. Despite the muscle cramps and his uncomfortable position, one thing did feel right.
The feel of Vivi's warm body nestled against
his as he listened to the rhythmic sound of her
breathing while she slept. He couldn't recall the
last time he'd felt such a deep sense of peace.

Was that because of all he'd told her about
himself?

There was no denying a feeling of calm and
catharsis had seemed to settle over him. For the
first time in a long while, he didn't feel tense or
wound up, like he constantly had to be on the
alert for the next catastrophe.

He had no idea how long it might last but
knew he had Vivi to thank. Somehow he'd
opened up to her about the most painful details
of his life and the world hadn't come crashing
down to an end. There'd been no judgment in
her reaction. No words of sympathy or—heaven
forbid—pity. She'd just listened.

He hadn't realized how badly he'd needed someone to do that.

His phone vibrated in his pocket and he felt the ding of several messages and emails downloading at once. Apparently they'd just regained cell service.

He had to check to see what those messages were. After the meeting with the Sevilles he was technically off the clock, had penciled time off to spend the day with Vivi. But his work never actually stopped. He couldn't just lounge here enjoying the feel of Vivi sitting on his lap for hours. As tempting as that was. Plus, a killer migraine was in the process of forming in the center of his head because of his awkward position against the wall.

He gently rubbed a hand down her cheek to rouse her awake. "Vivi, the storm has stopped. We can leave."

She stirred ever so slightly before settling back. Zeke took a moment to indulge himself in studying her. Long thick lashes as dark as midnight. Tanned skin kissed by the Southern sun. Ruby-red lips that she chewed absentmindedly from time to time when she was deep in thought.

He knew exactly what those lips tasted like.

Another text vibrated on his phone. He really

had to look at those messages. There might be something important that needed his attention.

He tried again to awaken her, rubbing his palm down her upper arms until she finally stirred. It took several moments but eventually her eyes slowly drifted open. Her lips thinned as she looked around in question.

She certainly looked adorable when she first woke up, all confused and flustered from sleep.

"It's done, sweetheart. The storm has moved on. We can finally get out of here."

She gave her head a brief shake and rubbed the drowsiness out of her eyes. "How long have we been in here?"

"I'm not quite sure. But I'd say it was long enough. We can head back to my place and relax by a fire after a nice hot shower."

That sounded like he intended for them to shower together, then cuddle up in front of his fireplace. He hadn't meant for it to sound so intimate. Not that the idea didn't sound down-right heavenly.

Vivi looked up at him then, the longing in her eyes so deep and clear that he felt the breath rush out of his lungs. Her desire was clear on her face and matched his own.

When she tilted up her chin to angle her face closer to his, he took it as the clear invitation it was. In the next instant, he was kissing her, his hands roaming over her luscious curves as he relished the feel of her hot breath in his mouth.

She turned to fully face him, straddling him in the process, and he thought he might die from the pleasure. She had the heart of an angel and more spirit than anyone he knew. He'd never met anyone like her, and she called to him on every level.

Sweet heavens, he wanted her. Like he'd never wanted any other woman in the past.

But they were in an abandoned castle propped up against a damp, cold wall. None of that would do.

There was no longer any denying where things were headed between them. But this wasn't the time. He wanted their time together to be right. Not rushed and frenzied under a leaking stone roof.

Somehow, he found the discipline to pull away and gently nudge her back. She blinked up at him in confusion and hurt. He couldn't have that at all. Cupping her chin, he brushed another soft kiss against her lips.

"You can't think I don't want you."

She blinked twice more.

"But not like this." He gestured around them. "Not here."

He knew he was making the right call. But, man, pushing her away like that had felt ever so wrong.

CHAPTER THIRTEEN

VIVI COULD STILL feel the warm flush on her cheeks as they loaded up the car with their carry-ons and drove away from the château.

Hard to tell if the heat on her face was due to the effects of Zeke's earth-shattering kisses or because of her horrified embarrassment. She'd practically mauled him back there, after throwing herself at him. How utterly mortifying that he'd been the one who'd had to pull away.

Not her classiest moment. But she didn't have too many of those.

"I can't believe we just spent part of the afternoon stranded in an old abandoned mansion," she said, just for some semblance of a conversation. Being in a tight car in such close proximity to Zeke after what had just happened was unnerving her and making her tense.

"There's quite a few of them dotted around the countryside and all throughout France."

"Oh?"

He nodded. "During the revolution, when the elite were forced to flee, they had to leave everything behind. Including their luxurious palace-style homes."

Of course, she remembered studying that period of history in school. "It must have been beautiful once."

"Maybe some wealthy retiree will buy it and fix it up."

"I hope so," Vivi answered. "The place did save us from a rather frightening storm. It deserves to be restored to its original grandeur."

An hour later, mostly spent in awkward silence, they pulled up to a quaint little cottage with a gravel road and small patch of grassy yard in the front. The house was surrounded by tall trees and thick, leafy bushes. It sat in front of a rolling hill dotted with yellow flowers. *Charming* was the first word that came to mind. "Do you rent this place or something when you're in town?" she asked as he slowed the car and came to a stop.

"I used to," he answered. "Then I just bought it outright to make things easier. About a couple of years ago."

Every time she seemed to turn around, Zeke did or said something to impress her even more than she already was by him.

"I have a service that comes in to maintain

and stock it for me regularly. There should be plenty to eat and drink."

Again, that sounded like him. No unplanned shopping trips, for Zeke's life was planned and orderly. Seemed to be working out well for him. He owned a cottage in the French countryside. Bessa and Vivi scrambled every month to make their rent and pay the utility bills.

He pulled out his phone and punched some keys on the screen. The garage door started to rise up, opening to reveal a tidy one-car bay area with wooden steps against the side wall leading to the main house.

Zeke came around to help her out of the car. "I, for one, can't wait to get out of these damp, filthy clothes," he told her.

Right. He'd mentioned showering. Was it her imagination or had he inferred that they'd be taking said shower together?

Her insides quivered at the thought. But she wasn't going to go making any assumptions. And she certainly wasn't going to make the first move after she'd practically attacked him back there upon awakening.

You can't think I don't want you.

As soon as they went up the steps and Zeke shut the door behind them, all her questions were answered and her doubts vanished. He pulled her toward him and crushed his mouth to hers in a hard, satisfyingly punishing kiss.

She could feel the strength of his desire, and it sent a feminine thrill down her spine. This enigmatic, compelling, attractive man wanted her. He couldn't take his hands off her. No one had ever made her feel this wanton, this desirable. She could let it go to her head if she wasn't careful.

Right now, however, it was time to throw all caution to the wind.

Her arms wound around his neck and she pushed closer to his length. She would never be able to get enough of him.

"Now," he whispered against her mouth, then took her hand and led her farther inside. "About that shower."

"We never did make it to the lavender fields," Vivi said an hour later, her voice wistful and sad. They were under the warm down comforter of his king-size bed. It was a far cry from the hard, cold floor and the stone wall they'd been forced to endure during the storm earlier. The shower had helped warm them up at first, though bathing hadn't exactly been the primary activity.

"Tomorrow is another day. Those flowers aren't going anywhere."

She ran a finger down his chest, sending desire surging through him once more. "So we'll go sometime tomorrow?"

"We can head there right after breakfast."

"Promise?"

It was hard to think with that wayward finger of hers running along his skin and tempting him all over again. "Absolutely. Though it pains me."

She lifted her head to look at him in question. "What? Why?"

He kissed the tip of her nose before answering. "Because, I'd much rather stay here. In bed. Just like this."

She grinned at him, like the cat who'd just gotten away with slurping up spilled milk. "We'll be sure to make it a very quick trip."

"It will have to be," he answered, gently nudging her on her back and settling over her.

He couldn't seem to get enough of this woman.

Remember, temporary, an unwelcome voice reminded him from the deep recesses of his mind. He pushed it away, focusing on Vivi's soft, luscious welcoming lips instead.

Temporary didn't have to mean short-term.

The aroma grew stronger and stronger the farther they drove. A rich flowery scent that reminded Vivi of expensive perfume. They had to be getting close.

Zeke confirmed it when he spoke. "Just about five more minutes."

A moment later he turned into a dirt road at the base of a tall hill. When they cleared the top, a sprawling complex of buildings came into view.

"Welcome to Roge Abbey."

When Vivi stepped out of the car after Zeke parked on a grassy knoll, she felt as if she'd crawled into a bottle of lotion.

"The tour will start in a few minutes," Zeke informed her. "But we can take a peek at the flowers first."

He led her down the side of the building and Vivi's breath caught in her throat after they rounded the wall. Rows and rows of rich, deep purple flowers that appeared to go for miles. "It's breathtaking," she said, overcome by the wonder she was looking at.

Again, the pictures she'd called up on her phone and on Zeke's laptop earlier hadn't quite caught the beauty of the scene before her. And, of course, the scent in the air wasn't something one could appreciate by reading about it.

"It's late June," Zeke said. "So we timed it right. Flowers are blooming and ripe with aroma."

Vivi inhaled deeply, savoring the exotic scent. "Careful," Zeke warned. "It can get overwhelming after a while."

Like the feelings she'd developed for him. The silly thought popped into her head and gave her pause. They'd shared an incredible night together. He'd held her like fine valuable china, been affectionate and gentle. Though there had also been those moments when he'd been less than gentle, but in the best of ways.

Overwhelming.

He continued explaining. "This is real lavender," he told her. "Only grown in very specific regions. Most of the world grows a different variety of flower. It's not the same thing."

"Like champagne versus sparkling wine."

He tapped her nose playfully. "Exactly like that."

Vivi bent down and rubbed her finger down the tiny, soft delicate petals. He was right—the flowers even felt different than the lavender she'd handled in the past. Smoother, like soft delicate velvet.

Zeke gently took her by the elbow to help her up when she began to straighten. "We should get to the main building," he said with a glance at his watch. "The tour's about to start."

She followed him back down the side path to the front of the abbey. Before they rounded the wall's corner, Zeke's phone rang.

"I don't mind if you get that," she told him, already rather guilt-ridden that he'd taken so much time out of his schedule just to play tour guide for her. She was only here because he'd needed her to help him out of an awkward business situation with the Sevilles. Their growing intimacy was another matter entirely.

His eyebrows drew together when he looked at the screen. "I think I will," he told her. "Go ahead on the tour without me if they start. I'll find you as soon as I'm done with the call."

Vivi couldn't resist planting a small peck of a kiss on his chin before she turned away and he clicked on the call. The day was already one for the scrapbooks. She'd woken up to find Zeke had surprised her by running out to fetch them a delicious breakfast of chocolate croissants and fresh baguettes smothered in brie. Along with rich, satisfying French-roast coffee. A girl could get used to such gestures.

Now they were here in this majestic abbey surrounded by so much beauty, it took her breath away.

She couldn't recall the last time she'd felt so content. So…dare she say it? So happy.

The day had just begun and she was going to enjoy every minute of it. In the company of the man she'd fallen in love with.

The thought had her stopping short. There was no denying it. Somehow, when she hadn't been paying attention, she'd fallen head over heels for

Zeke Manning. A man utterly wrong for her—the polar opposite of her free-spirit personality and hopelessly out of her reach. But, nevertheless, she was completely in love with him.

Not that she would ever be able to tell him that.

Zeke gripped the phone so tight in his hand it was a wonder the screen didn't crack. Bill Wolfson was calling him.

Why now, after all this time?

Zeke had figured that he hadn't found anything when he hadn't heard from the other man. Then he'd sort of forgotten that he'd even asked him to look into one Vivienne Ducarne of New Orleans, Louisiana.

But now Bill was calling. There was no other work he'd been doing for the firm. This call had to be about Vivi.

Zeke swore out loud, knowing he was going to regret answering. But he knew deep in his core that he had to. Sooner or later he would have to face what he was about to hear.

"Hey, Bill," he answered.

"First of all, I have to apologize."

"For?"

"I would have called you much sooner. But I had a bit of a family emergency."

"Is everything all right?"

"It is now. My kid had to have an emergency appendectomy. Then he had a bad reaction to the anesthesia. But he's fine now."

"I'm glad to hear it," Zeke said to be polite. But inside he was screaming for the man to get on with it already and explain the reason for his call.

"Anyway, I would have contacted you before with this information if it wasn't for all that."

"What information?" Zeke asked, though he could feel in his core that he didn't really want to know.

"You asked me to look into that young lady. I've sent a file to your inbox but figured I'd call as well."

Something shifted in Zeke's gut. A cold dread ran down his spine. He had an urge to pretend to lose the connection and drop the call. Then ignore the ring when Bill called back. But that would just be putting off the inevitable. Bill had found something in Vivi's past. Something she had kept from him. "What did you find out?"

The sound of Bill clearing his throat sounded through the tiny speaker. This was clearly going to take a while. Zeke leaned back against the door of the rental car and braced himself.

"She's got a pretty serious criminal history."

The breath rushed out of Zeke's lungs as the word pounded through his ear. *Criminal.* His investigator was informing him that the woman he'd been falling for was a criminal.

Bill continued, "Starting when she was a juvenile. But those files are sealed."

"And as an adult?"

"Let's just say I'm surprised she hasn't done any time."

"What exactly has she done? How serious?" Zeke asked, trying hard to ignore the loud pounding of his heart. His vision had gone dark, his palms had grown clammy with sweat.

"She was an accomplice in an armed robbery. That's pretty serious."

A young gentleman wearing a smock and beret-style hat greeted her when she walked through the abbey door, introducing himself as Rainier. She was one of half a dozen others taking the tour. After a quick introductory spiel about what to expect, Rainier began leading them down a long corridor to another door that led outside.

Vivi hesitated, wondering if Zeke might perhaps finish up the call and join her, but ultimately she decided to follow the others. Getting lost in a sprawling abbey would not be a good turn of events. And Zeke had told her to go on without him if need be.

The minutes ticked by as Vivi tried her best to listen and pay attention to everything Rainier was telling them. He talked about the monks and how they meticulously tended to the flowers, and how much prep the soil needed before each season. Even the properties of the plant that gave lavender its unique spicy scent.

But Vivi could hardly absorb much of it. Where was Zeke?

The phone call must have been important. Or some kind of emergency. Maybe she should head back and look for him to make sure everything was all right.

But she couldn't just walk away from the group. On top of being rude, she wasn't even sure which way to go. They'd meandered around the building, as well as a greenhouse, and through several rows of fields.

Still no Zeke.

Just when she thought she couldn't take it much longer, Rainier finally led them to a small gift shop and bid them *au revoir*. Vivi exhaled a sigh of relief. Was Zeke all right? What had happened to keep him from the tour?

The tour had ended by the entrance of the abbey. She ran outside to finally get some answers. There had to be a good reason why Zeke had just stood her up.

He was standing with his arms crossed, leaned up against the passenger side of the rental, when she stepped out the door.

"Hey, is anything the matt—" She didn't get the last word out. The look of utter contempt on Zeke's face stopped her in her tracks.

He had no idea who she was. She'd been lying to him all this time. About her past, her very identity. He didn't even know anymore what was false and what was real. Questions hammered in his brain. How much had she kept from him? What crimes had she committed where she hadn't been caught?

What had really happened with Esther's missing necklace?

She stared at him now in desperate confusion. Even now, though he wanted to kick himself, he couldn't help but think how beautiful she looked. How innocent and naive.

Looks could be so deceiving.

"Zeke?" she asked, her eyes clouded with questions. She looked genuinely concerned. But he couldn't be certain that it wasn't all part of the same act.

"Not here," he growled and flung open the driver's-side door. Leaning across the seat, he opened the passenger door for her and waited for her to get in.

"Please tell me what's going on," she pleaded, buckling her seat belt.

"We can talk when we get back home."

This was going to be a most uncomfortable forty-five-minute drive back to his cottage. Just as well. He would need at least that amount of time to calm down and gather his thoughts enough to form a coherent sentence or two.

They hadn't even been on the road for ten minutes when she whirled on him in her seat. "Please pull over. This is ridiculous."

He grunted at that. *Ridiculous* was one way to describe how he'd been acting. Letting down his guard, taking everything he'd been told at face value. Putting his trust in someone he didn't even really know.

What a fool she must have taken him for.

"Zeke. I am asking you to pull this car over right now so that we can talk about whatever has you so heated."

No hint of pleading or confusion in her voice now. She sounded determined and firm. Wow, she really was good.

Perhaps she was right. Maybe it was better to get this confrontation out of the way. He drove until they were next to an empty field and slowed to a stop. Without a word, he shut off the car then got out and sat on the hood.

Vivi appeared in front of him within seconds.

"What's going on?" she demanded. "Why are you acting like this?"

"I have a question for you before I answer

any of yours," he told her bluntly, earning a stunned gasp.

She crossed her arms in front of her chest, met him eye-to-eye. "What question would that be?"

"Tell me the truth about what happened back in New Orleans."

"I don't understand."

"I think you do. I think you've been acting a part this whole time. I think you took something that didn't belong to you and then had your friends help you cover it up."

Her mouth fell open and her skin turned the color of fresh snow.

"It's time you stopped lying to me, Vivi."

Vivi wanted to clamp her hands over her ears to keep from hearing anymore. Every word Zeke uttered landed like a physical blow. How could he be telling her these things? Asking her such accusatory questions?

She managed to find her voice, though her tongue felt heavy in her mouth. "Where is all this coming from?"

"I have an investigator who works for me occasionally. Does jobs for the law firm as needed. He found out some very interesting things when looking into your past."

She couldn't have heard him correctly. He'd been having her investigated all this time?

"You were paying someone to dig up dirt on me?"

"He didn't have to dig too deep."

Vivi couldn't believe what she was hearing. On wobbly legs, she paced in a circle as she tried to absorb exactly what was happening here. "When, exactly, did you hire him? Was it the day you kissed me for the first time? Did you call him between courses when we were having dinner in a tower overlooking Niagara Falls?"

"Don't be silly," he said, brushing off the questions. "I hired him that first day. When I first learned Esther had given you that darned necklace."

"But you never called him off. All the time we were together, you had someone out there looking into my past. You never put a stop to it even after…?" She couldn't even complete the sentence. It hurt too much to think about how intimate they'd been, given what he was doing to her right now.

"I'd say it's a good thing I didn't. You certainly weren't telling me about your past as an accomplice to armed robbery. Not even after I shared so much with you." The last few words hung in the air between them, full of accusation. He shook his head slowly, looked her up and down as if she was a worthless piece of litter he might have to step over in the street. Vivi felt the hot sting of tears behind her eyes.

"You don't understand. I had nothing to do with that. I was clueless about what he intended."

"He? Who? Ah, yes. The tattoo guy."

So he was going to be downright cruel about this. He wasn't even listening to what she had to say. "Yes. Him. He asked me to take him to the pawnshop because we were low on cash and he had some things that might sell. He asked me to wait in the car. Next thing I knew, Todd was running out of the building just as a squad car pulled up from behind with its lights flashing."

Zeke actually smirked at her. "So let me get this straight. You didn't know your boyfriend was inside robbing a business while you waited. And you also didn't know that you were in possession of a priceless antique after an old lady had given it to you."

"Yes! You know that was a simple misunderstanding."

He shrugged. "I know that's what you told me."

She literally stomped her foot in frustration on the soft, damp grass. "I told you that because it was the truth!"

"What about before?"

"Before what?"

"When you were younger. I've been told there's a sealed file."

"Wow. Your man did a very thorough job, didn't he?"

"It's why I pay him so well."

He'd paid the man to set up her betrayal. Her heart felt like it might shatter in pieces at the thought. "I had a young foster sister at one of the houses. The girl was being neglected. Barely given enough food, wore the same ragged sweater for days on end."

"What's that got to do with why you ended up with a juvenile file?"

"I took some things from a superstore so that she could eat and have clean clothes without holes in them."

Zeke tilted his head. She could tell by the curtain behind his eyes that her words held no weight whatsoever where he was concerned.

"How noble of you," he said, his voice dripping with sarcasm. "Did it occur to you to maybe notify someone? To get help of some sort?"

"You of all people should know better than to ask that. I was a teen, barely more than a child. Do you think anyone in a position to do anything was going to listen to someone like me?"

"So your first impulse was to break the law."

"I was a kid in a tough spot. I thought I had no choice."

"Why, Vivi? Why wouldn't you have told me any of this?" He rammed his fingers through his hair. "You had so many chances to come clean. Why keep it all from me if you're really as innocent as you say?"

Just the fact that he was asking such questions told her there was no answer she could give that would satisfy him. He'd already come to his conclusions. Nothing she told him now would make a lick of difference, not after what had just transpired between them by the side of this road.

Why should she even bother to try and defend herself? Zeke didn't care about what she had to say. His reaction right now was exactly the reason he hadn't confided in him about any of this. Her whole life, no one had ever had enough faith in her to believe anything she had to say. Zeke was no different.

But this time it *felt* different. Her heart felt shattered in her chest. She'd fallen for this man, had trusted her heart to him. And he was so ready to think the worst of her. Wasn't even giving her a chance to explain. Todd had betrayed her and taken advantage of her trust. What Zeke was doing was even worse. Because she loved him in a way she'd never felt for anyone.

Her legs had only grown wobblier, and it was hard to remain upright. But they were in the middle of nowhere in a field, and sitting on the hood of the car wasn't an option when he was already perched there. She refused to collapse to the ground. She wouldn't give Zeke the satisfaction.

"I'd like to go back now. I think this conversation is over."

He nodded briskly, jumped off the hood. "I agree. There's nothing more to say."

"I don't mean back to your cottage. I'd like to go back home to Louisiana."

She couldn't stand to be here in France with Zeke Manning for one more day, let alone under the same roof. She never should have agreed to come in the first place.

CHAPTER FOURTEEN

"EVEN FOR SOMEONE at a blues festival, you're looking particularly gloomy."

Against her better judgment, Vivi had allowed Bessa to convince her to come out to one of New Orleans's most popular summer events. An event she usually enjoyed every year. But not so much today. She was in no mood to be in a crowd of this many people, would much rather wallow by herself in front of the fan in their apartment. Lafayette Square was bursting with tourists and locals alike out to enjoy the day and hear the bands who'd come here to perform from all over the country.

"Sorry, Bessa. I have a lot on my mind."

Bessa sat back down on the bench next to her after dancing to the last song. Now they were waiting for the next set to begin, by a quartet called the Bayou Baritones.

"Girl. Just stop." Bessa gave her a nudge on her knee. "We both know you only have one thing on your mind. And it's not a thing at all. It's a who."

"That obvious, huh?"

"Wanna talk about it?"

"Aren't you tired of hearing me yet?"

Her friend gave her an indulgent smile. "Never. You know that."

She may not have been lucky in love, but Vivi had the greatest friends a girl could hope for. Bessa being top of the list.

"Maybe you should just call him," Bessa suggested, not for the first time. "Just get everything off your chest."

"I don't think it would do either of us any good. No, the best thing to do would be to move on. Forget I ever met the man."

"How do you plan to do that?"

Vivi sucked her bottom lip. "Just keep reminding myself of why it went so bad between us, I guess. Repeat in a continuous loop how different we are. How someone like me would never fit in the world a man like him inhabits. He would have never accepted me for who I am."

"What's that mean? Sounded like he accepted you just fine until that blasted investigator ruined everything."

Vivi shook her head with regret. "Not really. Zeke hired the man in the first place. And he never really did find me acceptable. One of the first times after we met, he said he couldn't understand why I wouldn't try and make more out of my singing."

Bessa clasped a hand to her chest in mock horror. "No! Not that! He paid you a compliment by saying you were good enough to try and go pro. Why, the man's a veritable demon!"

Vivi ignored the heavy sarcasm. "You know I'm not interested in pursuing any kind of professional singing career."

"Sure. For all the wrong reasons."

"What's that supposed to mean?"

Bessa turned in the bench to face her fully. "You don't want to call any attention to yourself. You want to lay low and stay out of any kind of spotlight. Because then people might figure out who you are and discover what happened in your past."

Vivi wasn't quite sure what her friend's point was. So what if all she'd just said was true? It made perfect sense. "Do you blame me? Look what happened with Zeke. As soon as he found out, he sent me back to the States in his jet while he stayed behind in France." That wasn't quite the truth. Vivi had demanded she fly back commercial, but Zeke wouldn't hear of it. He'd arranged for his jet and pilot to fly her back home while he'd returned to Manhattan on a commercial flight.

Bessa knew all that and sure enough, she called her on it. "The man arranged for a private flight for you because you demanded to leave."

"Fine," she begrudgingly admitted. Why did Bessa have such a strong recall of details? "None of that exonerates him."

"He was angry you didn't tell him the truth yourself. Whether or not he's justified in that is another story."

"And that's why you think I should call him?"

Bessa nodded. "Yep. You know what else I think?"

"What?"

"That you should rent out that sound studio uptown for an afternoon like you always talk about doing. And you should cut a track."

"And then what?"

Bessa threw her hands up in the air in frustration. "I don't know. Send it out to producers. Upload it to a streaming platform. How do aspiring recording artists get heard by the masses these days?"

Vivi squeezed her eyes shut. "I don't want to be heard by the masses. I don't want people to know who I am."

"That's not accurate, though. You don't want people to know what you did. What you did is not who you are. And you should tell this Zeke Manning that."

CHAPTER FIFTEEN

ESTHER SOUNDED GOOD on the phone. Zeke wasn't sure what to expect when he'd called her to follow up on the estate assessment, but to his relief, her voice came through clearly. She sounded alert and aware, so different than that fateful day he'd told her about the necklace two weeks ago back in New Orleans. He knew from speaking with various family members that she'd been receiving treatment from a team of neurologists and her prognosis was good in general.

Plus, apparently a grandniece who'd just gotten out of a messy divorce would be moving in with her for the foreseeable future. Hopefully, all of that meant no more priceless pieces of jewelry or antiques would be carelessly given away.

"I have to go, dear," she said now over the speaker of his office phone. "I have someone coming to the house in a few minutes. I'm going to have my cards done."

Zeke stiffened in his chair. She had to mean Vivi. Vivi was the one who made house calls to Esther to read her cards. Yet another reminder to jab at his wounds. Not that he needed any. Not that much time went by that he didn't think about her.

The last words they'd said to each other had been vicious and hurtful with no taking them back. He'd replayed the scene over and over in his head.

Esther continued, confirming what he'd suspected about Vivi's visiting her. "You met Vivi, didn't you, dear? Such a sweet girl. I had to find a way to pay her though she insisted no payment was necessary. I had to practically force that necklace on her that day. If only I'd known what I was actually giving the poor child."

With that, she clicked off the phone call.

Esther's words resonated throughout the walls of his mind—*had to practically force that necklace on her.*

Vivi had insisted on her innocence.

He'd never actually called up that cursed file to read it. There didn't seem to be any point. He'd heard all he needed to hear from Bill Wolfson.

What did it really matter what the file actually said? The end result would have been the same, wouldn't it? Vivi had a criminal record that she'd kept from him.

But now, curiosity was getting the better of him.

How had she been involved in an armed robbery, for heaven's sake? Without giving himself any time to think, he called up the email and downloaded the file Bill had sent him all those days ago. It only took reading one page to decide it was time for him to do some investigating of his own.

Less than twenty minutes later, Zeke knew two things for certain. One, he needed to call a recruiting firm to see about finding another PI for his business. And, two, he should have given Vivi the benefit of the doubt when she'd tried to explain everything that day by the side of the road.

Bill had only told him part of the story when he'd called Zeke in Provence.

It was all there in black and white. It had only taken a few clicks of a standard search engine to find news reports about the family Vivi had stayed with in foster care during the time in question. Years later, they'd been charged with neglecting the children in their care. So Vivi was telling the truth when she'd said she'd felt driven to steal.

Her actions hadn't been right. But her motives were pure and she was just a child.

As for the armed robbery, tattoo guy's real name was Todd Felton. In return for a lighter sentence, he'd turned in all the other criminals in his circle. But he'd steadfastly stuck to the same story about Vivi. That story being that she had no idea what he was up to in the pawnshop that day. The man would have had no motivation to say she wasn't involved if it wasn't the truth.

The guy was bad news, but at least in that sense, he'd done the right thing. And he'd stuck by it.

If only Zeke hadn't taken that phone call from the PI at the abbey. If he'd taken the time to look at the file the man had sent instead of answering the phone, he may have had time to process and think things through. He'd been so shocked and hurt that he hadn't been thinking straight.

He had to accept that Vivi hadn't actually meant to take Esther's jewelry. The truth of that was staring at him in digital format on his laptop screen and had been echoed in Esther's words just now in their phone call. He should have never accused her of outright theft and would regret it the rest of his life. It had been a heat-of-the-moment reaction based on the anger and shock he'd been feeling that day. Everything she'd been trying to tell him was verified by the file.

She should have been straight with him, but he should have given her a chance by the road in Provence to finally make that right. He could have handled it all so much better.

Zeke swore out loud and slammed his laptop shut so hard that the penholder on his desk fell over to the floor.

He'd been a fool. And he had to make it right somehow.

"Did the cards cooperate today, Vivi?" Lucien walked over to her table in the corner of the magic shop as Vivi gathered up her tarot set.

"They always do."

"You packing up for the day?" her boss asked.

"Yeah. I think I'd just like to get home." She'd had several walk-ins and the last client with an appointment had just canceled on her at the last minute. "Unless you need help closing later?"

Lucien shook his head. "Nah. Go get some rest. You've been looking kinda tired lately. If you don't mind my sayin'."

Lucien had never been one to pry, but Vivi knew he was always ready with a shoulder to cry on, if and when she needed it.

Vivi was done crying, though. She'd always carry a torch the size of a wildfire for Zeke

Manning, but she knew she had to move on. What's done was done.

They'd both done their part in wrecking what had sprung between them.

She should have been straight with him from the beginning, but he should have had more faith in her. Not to mention, the things he'd said and the words he'd used still stung like salt in a fresh wound every time she thought about the events in Provence.

Even if more than two weeks had gone by already. Every time she closed her eyes, she relived the scene by the field after the abbey tour. It was like picking at a scab, but she couldn't seem to help herself. Maybe she would stop doing that someday. No doubt about it, it was going to take a while to feel any kind of normal again.

Bending below the table to retrieve her pocketbook, she heard the chime of the front door, signaling the arrival of a customer. Vivi crossed her fingers and uttered a silent prayer that whoever had just arrived was a shopper in search of a souvenir and not here for a tarot reading. She really just wanted to get home and crash on the couch with a pint of praline caramel. But footsteps approached closer and closer until they stopped about eight inches away from where she was still crouched down.

Looked like she couldn't cut loose just yet. Pasting a reluctant smile on her face, she straightened to greet the newcomer.

Then did a double take at the sight that greeted her.

"Zeke?"

It couldn't be. Surely, she had to be seeing things. Her mind was conjuring what she wanted so badly. She rubbed her eyes just to be sure, but he was still standing there when she looked back up.

"Hey, Vivi."

Yep, it even sounded like him.

"What are you doing here?"

He pulled up the chair across from her table. "I was hoping to get a reading. If you have time, that is."

"You want a tarot reading? From me?"

"That's right." He pointed to the cards in her hand. "Is there a card in there that symbolizes a stupid, thoughtless man who should know better than to let the woman he loves get away?"

Vivi's heart felt ready to pound out of her chest. "The woman he what now?"

"Huh. I guess there's no such card, then."

She could only shake her head. "There's the Fool."

"That's close enough, I guess."

Lucien stood staring at them from the crystal-gemstone aisle, a knowing smile plastered on his face. Vivi had to wonder about the last-minute cancellation of her final client for the evening.

Zeke had taken the time and effort to arrange all this. Despite herself, she felt moved and touched.

Not so fast, a small voice cried the warning in her head. She couldn't let her heart be so open and vulnerable when it came to this man. She still hadn't recovered from the last time Zeke Manning had been careless with it.

"Here…" He reached into his jacket breast pocket, and to her utter surprise pulled out an engraved wooden box, like those custom-made to hold personalized tarot cards. It resembled a small treasure chest, complete with a copper key. "Use these."

She reached for the box with a shaky hand. "What are these?"

"I commissioned an artist to custom-make them for you. She dropped all her other projects to make these a priority."

Vivi gently opened the box and glanced at the signature on the cover card. A surprised gasp escaped her lips.

"Ranita Jackson drew these? She's the most sought-after visual artist in Louisiana. Maybe all of the South."

He nodded. "She said she'd make each card a work of art."

Vivi gently removed the deck, studied the delicate patterns and intricate details. Zeke was right—every card was an individual masterpiece.

"So what do you say? Are they telling you to forgive me?"

Vivi took a deep breath. As much as she wanted to jump into his arms, her heart felt heavy and weary. "I don't have to pull a spread to know what they should say."

He merely quirked an eyebrow.

She swallowed past the dryness in her mouth. "They'll say I should be careful, guarded." Heaven help her, she had to bite back a sob before she could continue. "They'll also say I can't handle being hurt that way again."

Zeke exhaled a deep sigh. "I can't deny any of that, sweetheart. I know how wrong I was to react the way I did."

"You didn't even give me a chance to defend myself. I'm not my past. I did what I thought was right and made some bad decisions in my lifetime. But I've learned from them and become a better person in the process."

He rubbed a hand down his face. "Vivi, I was an idiot back in France. I should have never forgotten even for a minute what a strong, willful and determined woman you are. I'll never forget again."

Well, he was certainly saying all the right things. Vivi took a moment to study him carefully. Dark circles colored the skin below his eyes and his hair was a mess of waves, as if he'd been running his hand through it repeatedly. He looked like he hadn't shaved in at least two or three days.

Maybe he'd been missing her as much as she'd been pining for him.

"What made you rethink this? Why did you come here, Zeke?" She had to know the answer, had to hear him say it.

He rammed a hand through his hair, only adding to the disheveled mess it already was.

"I was afraid, Vivi."

"Afraid?"

"Yes. Afraid of what I was feeling, afraid it wasn't real. That *you* weren't real. And then when I found out you'd been keeping things from me…"

She lifted a hand to stop him. He was right. But he'd never given her a chance to fix it or redeem herself. "I should have told you," she admitted, then had to suck in a breath before she could continue. "But I was afraid, too."

He gave her a wistful smile. "What a pair we make, huh?"

Vivi could only nod, at a loss for words.

"I promise to do better in the future," he told her. "If you'll just give me a chance."

Vivi couldn't take any more. She wasn't made of stone, after all. She'd really missed him. It had been so long. And now, here he was in the flesh. With a cry of resignation, she ran around the table and let him take her into his arms.

What she hadn't told Zeke was the true meaning of the Fool card. It meant new beginnings.

EPILOGUE

One year later

WHAT WERE THE odds of another freak thunder-storm striking in the exact same spot where they'd been caught last time?

Vivi ducked her head to look out the wind-shield of the convertible sports car as they made their way to the Sevilles' former estate. Zeke said he wanted to head out there to see how the transition was proceeding after his clients had taken over several months ago. He'd asked Vivi to accompany him so they could enjoy a com-plimentary wine tasting during their visit. He didn't have to ask twice.

Vivi could use the distraction. They were in town for her audition the next day for one of Europe's most popular vocal-audition shows. She still couldn't believe she'd actually made it this far in the process.

"I know it didn't help much last time, but did

you happen to check the forecast?" she asked. "The sky looks like it might be getting kind of dark."

Zeke looked away from the road just long enough to give her a wolfish grin. "If a storm hits again, we know exactly where to take shelter."

"I'd prefer to stay warm and dry, unlike last time."

Though she had to admit, waking up in Zeke's arms for the first time that day had not been without its merits.

"Afraid you'll be stranded and miss your audition?" He was joking, but just the mere thought of that happening had a brick settling in her stomach.

"Don't even jest about such a thing."

"You know, maybe we should stop at the abandoned château, anyway. Relive the past a bit," he added with a wink in her direction.

Vivi thought he'd made the comment as a flippant suggestion. But as they approached the structure, Zeke slowed the car and turned in the direction of the building.

"You're serious? I thought we were headed to the winery."

He came to a stop and killed the ignition. "We are. This will only take a minute."

Her confusion grew as they stepped out of the

car and several other vehicles appeared from down the road, eventually stopping near where they stood.

Utility trucks with construction equipment and an excavator. Several men climbed out of the vehicles and began unloading supplies.

What in the world was going on?

"Zeke?"

"The cottage is a bit small for both of us. And chances are good we'll be in France quite often. Especially when you win tomorrow night."

"*If* I win tomorrow." And it was a big if.

"When," Zeke insisted. "In any case, I thought we could use a bigger place."

Her mind didn't seem to be able to absorb exactly what was going on. And then it finally clicked. She felt her jaw drop.

"You—you bought an abandoned château? *The* château?" She stammered out the questions, too stunned to have her mouth work properly.

He nodded. "The renovations will take a while, but I think the wait will be worth it."

For one of the very few times in her life, Vivi found herself at a loss for words.

Before she'd recovered from the confusion of what was happening around them, he shocked her even further. Taking her hand, he pulled a small velvet box out of his pocket.

"We almost got married by mistake about a

year ago. Will you marry me for real this time, Vivienne Ducarne?"

Vivi's heart felt as if it might explode in her chest. She loved this man with every fiber of her being. Her mind played back to the scene in the chapel that afternoon in Niagara Falls, when the minister was ready to perform a marriage ceremony before realizing why they were really there. Zeke had called her his almost-wife.

She'd known, even then, that she'd somehow fallen in love with him. And she'd loved him ever since and always would.

"Yes," she answered with a breathless gasp, throwing herself into his arms. "Yes. I will be your forever wife!"

* * * * *

If you enjoyed this story, check out these other great reads from Nina Singh:

From Wedding Fling to Baby Surprise
From Tropical Fling to Forever
Her Inconvenient Christmas Reunion
Spanish Tycoon's Convenient Bride

All available now!